AMBUSH!

When the killer's form jumped up and stood silhouetted against the skyline, Ki hurled the *shuriken* star blade. It glinted in the moonlight, and when it struck the bandit's forehead, the man screamed, batted at his head and then crashed over in the brush, kicking in death.

Ki sprinted for the road, hoping to intercept the assailant's partner, before the man could reach Jessie. Too late. The killer had managed to slip up behind the two women, leap onto the wagon and put his gun to Jessie's head. . . .

— WESLEY ELLIS —

LONE STAR

AND THE
CALIFORNIA GOLD

JOVE BOOKS, NEW YORK

LONE STAR AND THE CALIFORNIA GOLD

A Jove Book / published by arrangement with
the author

PRINTING HISTORY
Jove edition / May 1991

ISBN: 0-515-10571-6

Jove Books are published by The Berkley Publishing Group,
200 Madison Avenue, New York, New York 10016.
The name "JOVE" and the "J" logo
are trademarks belonging to Jove Publications, Inc.

PRINTED IN THE UNITED STATES OF AMERICA

10 9 8 7 6 5 4 3 2 1

★

Chapter 1

It was a warm spring morning on Jessie Starbuck's huge Circle Star Ranch when a rider suddenly appeared on the horizon. Jessie and Ki were about to watch her bronc buster, Sid Shepherd, break a particularly powerful and wild roan stallion, and so they hardly noticed the new arrival until the cowboy cleared his throat.

"Miss Starbuck?"

Jessie twisted around to see the rider with his hat off and a letter in his hand. "Oh, it's you, Randy. Well, climb up next to me on this top rail and watch Sid make his ride. It ought to be something special."

"Yes, ma'am," Randy said, flattered that he would be invited to sit by Jessie, who was the richest and most beautiful woman in all of Texas. After all, he was just another bronc buster himself, who'd long aspired to work for the Circle Star Ranch.

Once seated beside Jessie, Randy said, "Got a letter marked 'URGENT' on it from the post office."

Jessie took the letter without even bothering to glance at the return address. She was much too interested in the contest that was about to take place in her breaking corral between Sid and the roan stallion.

1

"Thank you, Randy. But you needn't have come all the way out here to deliver this. I have a man that rides to town and back every day to pick up the mail."

"I know that," Randy said, barely unable to tear his eyes from Jessie because he found her so beautiful. "But your man doesn't come in for another couple of hours, and this letter, sayin' urgent and all, well . . . well I just thought you ought to have it right quick."

"Ear the son of a bitch down!" Sid shouted to his two helpers.

The roan stallion was snubbed to a stout post in the center of the corral and was fighting like crazy to break free. But it was blindfolded by a piece of gunnysack and no match for three experienced cowboys. The two Circle Star cowboys each grabbed an ear and twisted it like a dishrag. The roan was suddenly paralyzed with pain, and that's when Sid jammed his boot into his saddle, then swung aboard.

The bronc buster was a short, wiry man in his early twenties. Being top cowboy on the best ranch in Texas, he was openly arrogant and cocky. His huge Stetson was pulled down rakishly over his low brow, and he wore a pair of large, silver Mexican spurs that jangled as he sauntered toward the horse. Jessie didn't care for the young man, but she had to admit he had the quickness of a cat and the courage of a cornered badger.

"Let him go!" Sid yelled.

The two cowboys released their hold on the roan's ears, and at the same moment, Sid yanked the blindfold.

"Woo-wee!" Sid bellowed, lashing the dazed roan across the rump so hard his rawhide quirt drew welts the diameter of a rawhide reata. "Yee-haw!"

The roan exploded in a frenzy of anger and pain as Sid roweled it from just behind the shoulder clear back near its haunches. Jessie's eyes narrowed with disapproval as she saw hair and hide tear away from the roan and be replaced with streaks of blood.

The roan went straight up in the sky, its nostrils red and flared, its eyes rolling like dice in a cup. When the roan came down, it did so straight-legged, and everyone watching saw Sid's chin strike his chest and then whip back as the roan went skyward again.

"Look at that big son of a bitch buck!" a cowboy swore, forgetting that Jessie did not condone such talk.

Jessie, however, did not hear the man. She had been raised on this ranch and she knew horses and how they ought to be broken. In this case, she was upset by what she considered unnecessary savagery. The roan's flanks were being ripped by the bronc buster's rowels.

"Git after him!" another cowboy shouted, as the roan bucked, almost unseating its rider before it charged across the corral, struck the far wall and cracked poles in its effort to crush Sid's legs and rid itself of the man on its back.

"Watch your legs!" Randy yelled.

The roan made two more spectacular leaps into the sky and then again landed stiff-legged. Sid's head snapped down and then whipped back up as the roan catapulted skyward. It seemed to Jessie that the only thing that was keeping the man aboard the horse was those locked spurs. Sid's nose was bleeding profusely. He had lost his hat and didn't seem to have the strength to use his quirt.

The roan sensed the man weakening. It charged the fence, again willing to inflict harm and injury upon itself if it could crush the hated rider.

"Ahhh!" Sid screamed as he tried and failed to pull his leg up and over his saddle horn.

Randy leapt from the top pole of the corral and raced forward hearing men shout a warning into his ear. He lunged at

3

the roan, which was, by now, completely crazed by pain and fury. The roan spun and its right front hoof whacked Randy across the side of the head, knocking him out cold.

Jessie also left the top rail and, heedless of her own safety, raced in with several others, grabbed Randy by the arms and dragged him out of the center of the corral just in time to see the roan rear up into the air.

"Bail out!" Jessie shouted in warning as the horse teetered on its hind legs.

But Sid was dazed and unable to think clearly, and Jessie stood helplessly by as the roan crashed over backward, coming down on the pole corral fencing.

It was over in a split second. Sid didn't even scream as he was impaled on his saddle horn and the roan broke its neck in the splintered fencing.

"Oh my God!" Jessie cried, grabbing ahold of the quivering roan and trying to pull it off of her bronc buster.

In a matter of seconds, no less than five Circle Star cowboys were in the corral, all of them pulling the horse off the man.

"He's gone, Miss Starbuck," a cowboy said. "He musta died instantly, just like that goddamn crazy son of a bitch that killed him."

Jessie steadied herself against the shattered pole corral. She had seen a great deal of death in her life. Tragedy was part of the human existence out here on the Texas frontier. But the violence of this encounter had left her shaken, and the most terrible thing was that none of it had been at all necessary.

"Are you all right?" a cowboy asked.

"Yeah," Jessie said, removing her Stetson and sleeving perspiration from her forehead. "Did Sid have any relatives that you know of?"

The cowboys all looked around at each other, and a man

named Pete, who had been Sid's closest friend, shook his head. "He was a loner, Miss Starbuck. Sid never married or had children."

"What about a mother or a father?"

"He never said anything about 'em," Pete told her. " 'Cept once when he mentioned that he wished he'd never been born in Baltimore. I sorta got the idea that he ran away from home when he was little more than a colt."

Jessie shook her head. Sid's chest was crushed and there was blood everywhere. "We'll bury him within the hour," she said. "We'll put him in the Starbuck Cemetery along with my mother and father, and every other cowboy that has died in my employ."

The cowboys nodded. One of them looked up through the broken corral fence and said, "Here comes Ed and Ki."

Jessie was glad to hear that. Ed Wright was her foreman and had been for many years. Her father, Alex Starbuck, had hired Ed when he was a young cowboy, and Ed had proven his worth ever since. A tall, slow-moving but very knowledgeable cowman, Ed could have long ago built a successful cattle ranch of his own from the generous salary he was paid, but he liked to work for Jessie as much as he'd liked working for Alex.

Ki was the first to reach her. Half-Japanese and the son of an American sailor, Ki was a samurai and was Jessie's best friend and confidant. He was also her protector, the man that made sure that she was not hurt or attacked by someone crazy enough to think that he could cash in on the Starbuck fortune.

The samurai was not one to ask stupid or irrelevant questions. "We'll have him ready for burial within forty minutes. You don't have to . . . "

"Yes I do," Jessie said, "and I want to say a few words of my own when we lay Sid to rest."

5

"Miss Starbuck?"

Jessie turned to her foreman. "Yes?"

"Randy is knocked out colder than an icicle. Might even have a concussion. He's bleeding from the scalp and from his ears, ma'am."

Jessie hurried over to kneel beside Randy. He was her own age, early twenties, tall and slender. Jessie recalled very well how, as a boy, he'd been awkward, but now that he was filling out, Jessie could see that he was going to be a fine looking specimen of manhood with his square jaw, blue eyes and sandy hair.

"Randy," Jessie said, "can you hear me?"

The young man showed no signs of recognition, and Jessie thumbed back his eyelids. Her heart sank. "His pupils are dilated. Send a man on a fast horse to get Doc Withers."

Ed quickly chose a cowboy to make the seven mile ride, and then he, Ki and a couple other men grabbed Randy and carried him inside the huge ranch house, which the late Alex Starbuck had called home, even though he'd owned several villas and estates around the world.

"Put him in the upstairs bedroom next to mine," Jessie said, hurrying into the kitchen to order her house staff to heat water and make bandages.

When Jessie went back upstairs, Randy was stretched out on the bed. He was very pale and his skin was cold.

"Let's get him in bed," Jessie told her men.

"Are you going to sew that up?" Ki asked.

"I'd better. He's losing a lot of blood."

Ki nodded. He'd often seen Jessie doctor men, horses, dogs, cats and cattle. She kept surgical needles and other instuments in a cabinet in her kitchen, and a good supply of surgical gut for just this sort of accident.

"I'll get what you need," the samurai told her as he hurried out of the room.

"You need us to help?" Ed asked.

Jessie shook her head. "Why don't you go and see that Sid's body is being taken care of properly. And as for the dead bronc, get some of the men to rope and drag it out on the range."

"I wish I could have been here when it happened," Ed told her. "But me and Ki were checking the south fence and . . . "

"And even you couldn't have done anything to prevent the accident," Jessie told him.

"I saw the roan's flanks." Ed shifted uncomfortably. "They looked like Sid was using a pair of butcher knives on that roan. What happened?"

Jessie sighed. "He must have sharpened and locked up the rowels on those big Mexican spurs. When I saw the way he was opening up that roan's flanks, I was horrified. Sid knew I wouldn't tolerate treating even an outlaw stallion that way."

"Maybe figured that he was gonna get piled if he didn't lock his spurs."

"Maybe. But that didn't give him an excuse to sharpen the rowels. Ed, I feel terrible about losing Sid, but to be honest, I'd have fired him after that ride. I won't have a man that gets vicious with a bronc. He can be rough because that's required, but never cruel."

"Well," Ed drawled, "it looks like Sid paid for his mistake."

"I'm afraid so. Let's just hope that poor Randy doesn't also pay with his life."

"By the way," Ed said, "one of the boys found this letter out in the corral. It was marked 'URGENT,' and you musta dropped it when you jumped off the rail."

Jessie took the letter and glanced at the envelope. "Yes, I remember now. Randy brought it all the way from town."

7

"Don't he know we pick up our mail every day?"

"I think he was just looking for an excuse to ride out. He's been wanting to bust broncs for me for the last year or two. But when I asked Sid about him, he said Randy wasn't good enough."

"Maybe there was bad blood between them. You know bronc busters are a breed all unto themselves. They're always competing to see who's the best. My guess is that if Sid didn't like Randy, it was because he was afraid the young fella might show him up and prove himself better."

"I was thinking the same thing," Jessie said, glancing at the return address and noting it was from a town called Pineville, in California. As far as Jessie could remember, she knew of no one in a town of that name.

Stuffing the dirt-stained envelope and letter into the back pocket of her man's Levis, Jessie turned when Ki entered the bedroom with her medical supplies.

"Ed, you and Ki had better each grab an arm and hold on tight," she said. "This won't feel good and he's likely to react strongly."

"We'll hold him still," Ki promised as he watched Jessie thread the gut though a hooked surgical needle, which she handled with a pair of steel forceps.

Jessie laid the forceps and needle down on the bedside, and when her housekeeper bustled into the room with bandages and hot water, Jessie said, "Put it right here on the table, Willa. Thank you."

"Anything else you need?"

"Just say your prayers. Randy is a fine young man and I won't have him die."

Jessie wasted no time in cleansing the wound. She tried to stop the flow of blood, but the wound was deep, about three inches long over the right ear.

"I'm just glad he wasn't struck in the face," she said as much to herself as to her men. "He's a handsome young fella, and it would probably have broken some girl's heart."

"You're the only girl he's been interested in since he was sixteen," Ed told her grim-faced.

Jessie picked up the forceps and needle. "What are you talking about?"

"Just that Randy has a sweet spot for you about the size of Texas."

"I don't believe that. Why, he's never even suggested . . ."

"What's to suggest? He's just a cowboy. A bronc buster, true enough, but that business ain't known for makin' men rich."

Jessie frowned. With her shapely figure, green eyes and strawberry-blond hair, she was the kind of woman that turned heads. Still, she never thought of her self as classically beautiful. She just tried to be smart and to run the Starbuck empire as her father would have had he not been assassinated by an evil international cartel.

"Hang on to him tight," she ordered as she bent close and hooked the needle through Randy's scalp.

The young man bucked like a wild horse and his eyes opened, but they were wild and unfocused. For a moment, he almost broke free, and then Ki, with his Oriental wisdom and the ancient knowledge of the samurai, used *atemi* on him. *Atemi* was the application of enough pressure to momentarily arrest the flow of blood to the brain, causing instant unconsciousness.

"If he wasn't out before, he sure is now," Ki said. "So go ahead and sew him up."

"Thanks," Jessie said, taking care to space her sutures as neatly as if she was doing some fine sewing.

Jessie had a gift for being able to concentrate totally on

whatever task was at hand. Now, she sutured up the bronc buster as neatly as any practicing surgeon and cut off the bleeding completely.

When the suturing was finished, she leaned back and surveyed her handiwork and then thumbed back one of Randy's eyelids. "I still don't like it," she said. "I think he's had some brain damage."

Neither Ki nor Ed made any comment, and when their work was over, they both went out to oversee the burial and removal of the roan stallion.

Jessie moved over to the window and watched. It was a tragic day for certain, and if Randy also died or was permanently brain damaged, she would never forgive herself.

Placing her hands on the small of her back and stretching, her fingers brushed the letter. The damned letter that had brought Randy to this sad and unconscious fate. Jessie reached for the letter and tore it open to read it aloud.

"Dear Jessie, I know that it has been years since we last were together in San Francisco. I acted like a fool that day because I was so madly in love that, when I learned you did not share my love, I became crushed and embittered. I left the city and went prospecting for gold. Yes, gold! Can you imagine a teacher, a lover of the classics, grubbing about for gold?

"Well, I ended up here in Pineville, and I bought a weekly newspaper. I am supremely happy, though still a bachelor. So why am I writing you an urgent letter? It is because I desperately need your help. These beautiful Central Sierra Nevada Mountains are in danger of becoming slag and mud heaps because of hydraulic mining. Only with your help can the ruthless Tower family be stopped from destroying this beautiful country.

"You *must* come and help us, Jessie. And by all means, bring Ki! Hurry please if you value my devotion and friendship. And also if you value my life. Sincerely, Max Max-well."

Jessie frowned and gazed out her window. Max had been desperately in love with her, and she had also felt a strong attraction to him. But she had not wanted to get married, and Max had insisted on living in California, a state which she liked to visit but which would never replace Texas in her heart.

Jessie studied the letter again. Was Max's life really in jeopardy? He was a romantic and this sort of thing was theatrical enough to appeal to his imagination. Also, he might have believed that except to rescue his life, she would not drop her affairs here in order to come.

"How can I be sure?" she whispered. "And what if his life really is in danger and I ignore the plea?"

Jessie knew that she could not afford to take the chance that Max was exaggerating the state of affairs. Besides, she had heard of the terrible destruction caused by hydraulic mining, which was capable of blowing entire mountains down with its high pressure streams of water.

I will have to go to this Pineville in California, she decided—right after I bury my old bronc buster and am sure that my next one is going to survive.

★
Chapter 2

Jessie closed the Bible she had just finished reading a passage from and studied the fresh mound of dirt. A few personal words, she knew, were required. Taking a deep breath, she raised her head and studied the more than sixty employees of the Circle Star Ranch.

"Sid Shepard was a man who kept pretty much to himself. He had few friends, no family that anyone knows of. But the important thing to remember is that he had pride in what he did—and what he stood for. I'm not saying that I approved of how he handled that roan stallion, but he did the best he could. It just all worked out wrong."

Jessie expelled a deep breath. "As many of you remember, we buried my father and mother here, and both were cruelly cut down years before their time by an evil cartel—a gang of rich killers and madmen who wanted nothing less than to take over the world's financial markets and gain an economic stranglehold over humanity. My father fought that and it cost him his life. And Sid, he fought a horse and lost his life. One situation is much like the other—a willingness to sacrifice for values and beliefs. It's a noble reason for living—or dying."

Jessie turned and walked away. At the grave of her father

and mother, she stopped and laid two red roses in their memory. Her mother had died when she was so young that she scarcely remembered anything about the woman. But the memory of her father was sharp and very dear. Alex Starbuck had been an extraordinary man. He'd started out in life with nothing and saved enough money to buy a small import-export business in San Francisco. He had prospered and eventually purchased a ship and then steel mills and factories, plantations in South America and railroads around the world.

Everything that Alex Starbuck touched had turned to gold because of his hard work, integrity, vision and talent. But success had bred envy and then hatred, and that, in the end, had cost the empire builder his life.

Jessie bent and smoothed her father's grave. "You led your life according to your beliefs, too," she whispered before she stood and walked alone to her house, where she would turn her mind exclusively to helping young Randy recover and then preparing for her trip to a place called Pineville.

Two days later, the doctor finished his examination of Randy, who was still unconscious, and said, "I can't understand why he doesn't come out of his coma. If there were bleeding inside his skull, his pulse would be shallow and his color bad. But both are normal. He exhibits all the normal reflexes of a healthy human being. His muscles contract when they are pinched. He flinches at pain. And yet. . . . nothing."

"Isn't there something that can be done to bring him out of this?"

The doctor sighed. He was in his seventies, well respected because he had always tried hard to keep up with medicine and read every page of his medical journals. "Miss

Starbuck, sometimes the only thing that will heal the body is time. That, or some powerful stirring or sensation."

"Such as?"

"Pain . . . or pleasure."

Jessie blinked. The doctor looked tired and discouraged. "By the way," he said, "your suturing technique is excellent."

"Thank you. I've had plenty of practice on both men and animals."

The doctor nodded. "I think I had better be returning to town. Mrs. Freeman is expecting her first baby any moment now, and I'd like to stay close. She's a small woman with a very large husband. That can be a fatal combination during childbirth."

Jessie knew very well that the poor woman was under five feet tall while her husband was over six feet. "I'm sure it can."

"Someone told me that you might be going to California."

"Yes," Jessie said, "an old friend seems to be in trouble."

"So you and Ki are the ones that will bail him out, is that right?"

"We will try. His trouble has something to do with hydraulic mining. I've never seen it, but I hear it is a devastating practice."

"I wouldn't know," the doctor said. "Here in Texas, that is one scourge that we will never have to worry about. Instead we endure blizzards, Indians and tornados."

Jessie walked the man to the door. Doc Withers had been a longtime family friend and she'd known him since her earliest childhood. The doctor had once saved her father's life by pulling an arrow out of his side, and he'd saved the lives of many of her cowboys. Lately, he'd been talking about retiring and moving to San Antonio. Jessie suspected that he was even now seeking a young partner to take over his medical practice. The doc was not a man who would abandon his patients without a competent replacement.

Outside, a Circle Star employee had the doc's horse and buggy ready and waiting. The doc slowly climbed into the buggy, took his reins, then looked down at Jessie.

"If you need to go to California, then have your men bring Randy into town. I can put him up at Mrs. McAllister's boarding house until we see if he's going to recover or not."

Jessie's expression was grim. "I feel responsible for this. If Sid hadn't used that roan stallion so violently, I don't thing any of this would have happened. I should have fired the man some time ago, when his rough methods first came to my attention. But I only warned Sid instead, and now, look at the tragedy that has resulted."

"It's not your fault," Doc Withers said. "And as for Randy, the only thing we can do is wait and pray."

"Or see that he experiences great pain or pleasure." Jessie looked up at the doctor. "Isn't that what you said?"

"Yes, but who's going to inflict pain on an unconscious man?"

"No one," Jessie said absently. "Thanks, Doc, and don't work so hard. Tell Mrs. Freeman that I'm sorry I couldn't drop by for a visit, but I must leave for California at once. Tell her I'll come by the moment I return."

"I'll do that."

Jessie turned away and headed back to the house. She made a note to have one of her housekeepers go to town and buy Mrs. Freeman a present for her and the baby.

Ki was waiting for her on the porch. He was dressed in a loose-fitting black outfit, appearing fit and as calm as always. "When will we leave?"

"I'm not sure," Jessie said. "I can't go away leaving Randy unconscious, and yet, Max would not have written me from California unless the situation was indeed quite urgent."

"I will be ready whenever you are."

On impulse, Jessie said, "Ki, you've seen many men killed and injured. Do you think that young bronc buster has permanent brain damage?"

The samurai shook his head. "No. His pupils are still dilated, but everything else about him is normal. I think the brain was injured and is healing right now. But, of course, that is not a professional opinion."

"Thank you," Jessie said with relief. "You may not be a doctor, but you're generally correct about such things."

That night, Jessie could not sleep. Like her father, she had always prided herself on being a decisive person. Vacillation was a curse, and it inflicted little but worry and more doubts. But now, with Randy unconscious in the room beside her and dear Max in mortal danger in California, Jessie was torn with her desire to help both men.

Sometime after midnight, she arose from her bed and walked over to the window and pulled the curtains aside. There was a great full moon hanging against a cobalt sky. The stars were bright, and from far out on her range, she could just hear the faint chorus of a pack of coyotes making prairie music.

Slipping a silk bathrobe on over her white satin nightgown, Jessie left her room and went to look in on Randy. His breathing was easy and regular, and his pulse was strong and steady. She felt his forehead and there was no fever. He looked peaceful and almost serene asleep in the bed, and yet . . . yet Jessie could not help but agonize over the state of his mind.

"Extreme pain or pleasure," she whispered.

Jessie peeled back the covers and studied the young bronc

buster's body. Randy was tall and slender, really quite the perfect picture of manhood.

"All right," she said to herself, "since I can't administer pain, let's try the pleasure."

She unbuttoned Randy's pajamas and her long fingers slipped down to his flaccid rod, which she began to rub softly. To her relief and delight, he quickly grew long and hard.

"I wonder if you know what you are in store for now," she said, undressing quickly. For a moment, she stood poised beside the unconscious cowboy, her beautiful body silvery in the moonlight, before she bent and took his manhood in both of her hands and lowered her head, taking Randy into her mouth.

He groaned as Jessie worked skillfully over him for several minutes until his hips were thrusting powerfully.

"Randy," she whispered, "come back to us!"

He sighed and his mouth formed a small smile, but his eyes did not open. Jessie climbed over him, then guided his thick, wet tool into her lush honey pot and slowly eased down on the man, pulling his face to her large breasts.

His body responded just as she hoped it would, and she began to rotate her hips around and around on him until his breathing came fast and his hands actually lifted to cup her thrusting buttocks hard to his body.

"Randy!" she breathed into his ear. "Come back to me!"

His hands pulled her powerfully to his hips, and his body began to hammer upward at her so that she felt she was riding a young stallion. Faster and faster he moved until his eyes opened wide and he cried out in ecstasy and filled her with his seed.

"Miss Starbuck!" he cried. "Oh, Miss Starbuck!"

Jessie clasped him to her and felt her own passion explode

like a Chinese rocket as she milked him dry.

Jessie held the young bronc buster tightly and listened to her heart hammer in her chest.

A long time later, he rolled over onto her, and when she looked up into the moonlight, she saw that his handsome young face was wet with tears.

"Is this a dream?" he said quietly. "Is this the dream I've had all these years?"

"It's no dream," she told him. "It's just a woman trying to help a man she very much likes and admires."

"I don't want to wake up if it's a dream," he told her. "I never want to wake up again."

Jessie's thighs tightened around his hips, and she reached down and stroked his buttocks. "When the night is over, I'll be leaving and so will you."

"Where are you going?"

"To California to help save the life of an old friend."

"And where am I going?"

"To my bunkhouse. You're going to be my new bronc buster, aren't you?"

"Yeah," he said, "if you want."

"I want." Jessie laughed softly in her throat. "I am so happy that you are going to be all right."

"I feel like I've been sleeping a million years."

"Just a few days," she told him.

"Can I make love to you until morning?"

"I'd be disappointed if you didn't," she told him. "But after tonight, never again."

"But. . . . "

"Please," she said. "This must be our secret. Can I have your word of honor you'll never tell anyone and that you'll find a young woman of your own to love?"

He swallowed noisily. "After you, who could compare?"

"There are many girls who would love to love you," Jessie told him. "You just have to look for them. You have to forget about me."

"But why!"

"Because," she said, "I am Jessica Starbuck."

The young bronc buster nodded sadly. "Then I'm going to keep telling myself this is a wonderful dream. And that when I wake up tomorrow, the dream will be over but never forgotten."

Jessie smiled. "Make love to me again, please. I want you on top and awake for every minute of the rest of this night."

Randy smiled and his mouth found her breasts. Jessie sighed with pleasure, and soon their bodies were surging together as naturally as the ocean waves against a white sandy beach.

Jessie never quite knew how Ki anticipated her wishes, but he did again the next morning. All she had to do was to step outside wearing her riding clothes, with her saddlebags in one hand and a Winchester in the other, and Ki was ready to leave.

"Our horses are ready and waiting," Ki said as they moved across the ranch yard toward the livery barn.

Inside the barn, Jessie's palomino gelding, Sun, was stamping the earth impatiently. He had obviously been curried to shine, and Ki's pinto was equally well groomed.

Jessie shoved her Winchester into her saddle boot and tied her saddlebags down tight behind her cantle. "We'll ride directly over to El Paso and leave our horses there, then take the stage to Tucson and on to Tonopah, then up to Reno. From there, we'll get directions on how to find Pineville."

Ki nodded. "It will take more than a week."

"I know," Jessie said. "It's going to be a long, hard journey and we'll be crossing some hard country. I just hope the Paiutes are not on the warpath again over in Nevada."

When Jessie and Ki rode out of the barn, Ed Wright was standing in the ranch yard waiting.

"Spring roundup will be over in another three weeks," he said.

"You want me to hold the herds for market until you return?"

"Keep them until the end of June," Jessie decided, "and if I'm not back by then, drive them north. Also, telegraph my office in San Francisco and tell them to have money waiting for me at the Overland Hotel in Reno. Also, see if they can find out anything about the Tower family. They are apparently blasting away the Central Sierras with hydraulic mining. Tell San Francisco I want everything they have on that family as well as hydraulics, and I want it waiting for me at the Overland."

"No first handle to go with the Tower family name?"

Jessie pulled Max Maxwell's letter out of her Levi jacket and studied it once more. "No," she said, "there's no first name. But I have a feeling that, in California at least, this family is very well known—for all the wrong reasons."

Ed nodded. "What about the rest of your international operations?"

"Bill Fellows in San Francisco has my complete trust, and he knows what to do in my absence. I feel almost as confident about him as I do you, Ed."

Ed reached up and took her hand. "You know that we'll all be worried until you come back. So don't keep us waiting. Send a letter or a telegram if you're going to be delayed, and if you need anything then. . . . "

"I know," Jessie said with a smile. "Just hollar and the whole damn crew will come runnin'."

Ed blushed. "I guess I'm as bad as an old woman when it comes to worrying."

"I like you to worry about me," Jessie confessed. "You and Ki are my father and my brother. You're all the family I have now."

Ki secretly smiled inside with pride. Jessie was his reason for being a samurai. She was his purpose for living. He would never possess her like a man does a woman but, instead, would devote himself to her protection and happiness.

Ed walked around to the samurai's horse. He studied the warrior's unusually shaped bow and quiver of arrows. He knew that the samurai had secret weapons inside his jacket that could kill men damned every bit as fast as a gun. "Take care of yourself," Ed told the warrior.

"I am not important," Ki said. "But I will take care of Jessie."

"Hell you aren't important!" Ed scoffed. "Who else could I beat in poker if it wasn't you!"

Ki allowed himself a smile. Although he did not gamble for money, he did occasionally indulge in games of chance to test his skill against others. Cards, however, were not something he had a knack for, and he almost always lost, to the great amusement of men like Ed Wright who had been playing faro, poker and craps since they were boys.

Before Jessie turned away, she glanced toward window of the bedroom where Randy had recovered. He was standing in his working clothes, watching her with a sad smile. She returned his smile and wished she could blow him a farewell kiss, but of course, with half of her cowboys watching their departure, that was out of the question.

"Randy will take Sid's place as our bronc buster," Jessie said to her foreman.

"*If* he recovers."

Jessie's full lips formed a happy smile. "He had a miraculous recovery last night. This morning, he is frisky as a colt and we talked about his philosophy of breaking mustangs."

"Which is?"

"You break them without breaking their spirits," Jessie said, her eyes pulled back to Randy. "You handle a young, green horse like you handle a wild boy or girl. With firmness but with kindness and patience."

Ed followed her eyes to the window, and when he saw Randy watching them, he waved. "You're right. He looks rarin' to go."

"He is," Jessie said, the memory of their night of frenzied lovemaking very fresh in her mind.

Jessie waved to her cowboys, and then she and Ki reined their horses around and headed west—toward El Paso and then all the way to Reno and over the Sierras to a place called Pineville.

★

Chapter 3

Despite her first day's fatigue and the urgency of their mission, Jessie found herself enjoying their long journey to California. She and Ki had traveled all over the West together as well as around the world. But there was nothing as uplifting and satisfying as riding across wide-open frontier in the springtime when the wildflowers were in bloom and the land seemed to rejoice in its annual new awakening.

Even West Texas, normally arid, was colorful and alive with birds and wildlife. They saw deer and antelope by the score, and Jessie, who was an expert shot, kept them well fed. Every night, she would help Ki prepare simple but wholesome fare, and when their campfire burned low, they would roll up in their bedroll and stare up at a sky that was studded with midnight diamonds.

One of the stories about Ki that Jessie most enjoyed hearing was about the great Hirata who had saved Ki's life and taught him *kakuto bugei* , the true ways of the honorable samurai.

"He was huge," Ki said, as he reminisced the last night before they reached El Paso. "You see, after my father died and my mother was banned in disgrace for marrying an outsider, she could not support either herself or me. Soon, she

25

died of a broken heart and I was left to fend for myself. I was very young, and being of mixed blood, I was also tainted with disgrace. Other children ridiculed me and grown men spat in my path. Only Hirata would treat me like something more than a leper."

"And yet," Jessie said, remembering, "you told me that Hirata considered himself to be a man who lived in disgrace."

"Yes," Ki said quietly. "You see, when a samurai's master dies, the samurai considers his own life to be over because it is his purprose to serve a master."

"Couldn't he find another?"

Ki shook his head. "I am afraid even a great warrior like Hirata could not. You see, he could not ask, and no master would dare insult his own samurai by taking a great warrior who had fallen to the place of a *ronin*, which means a 'wave man,' a person who has no place and whose life is as rootless as the storm-tossed waves on the sea. But no matter how desperate Hirata's situation, he would never commit *budo*."

"What does that mean?"

"It means," Ki said, "that men without honor would come to Hirata, and because he was a great warrior, they would offer to pay him so that he might teach them *kyusutsu*, *kenjutsu*, *bojutsu* and *shuriken-jutsu*, the arts of bow and arrow, sword, staff and throwing knife, and the use of all the other fighting weapons."

"Even starving, Hirata would not accept payment?"

"No," Ki said. "The only reason he took me was that I had nothing to give. Nothing but my heart. And so, for the last years of his life, he took a thin, starving boy, an outcast—as he was—and taught him all the samurai's ways and fighting skills. And when I was a samurai, trained even in *ninjutsu*, the art of the invisible assassin, then he died."

"I am sorry for this."

"Don't be," Ki said. "Hirata died well. Even the greatest samurai in Japan were proud of his *seppuku*, which means suicide by ritual disembowelment."

Ki had once described the act, and it had left a lasting impression on Jessie's mind. According to the samurai's code, *seppuku* was a self-administered ritual. The samurai was expected to disembowel himself very precisely with two deep cuts, one vertical, one horizontal. He was not to cry out or lose consciousness before the cuts were made, and he was to maintain his composure until the instant of his death.

Jessie could not imagine how anyone could do this— much less keep from screaming in agony. Wanting to change the subject, Jessie said, "I think Hirata must have seen what my father saw in you, Ki. He saw honor and courage. He saw loyalty and intelligence. I would not have lived nearly so long except for your presence."

In the darkness, the samurai blushed with embarrassment. "A samurai does not expect or deserve compliments."

"You are wrong," Jessie said, "but you're too stubborn to admit it."

"No one ever said that even a samurai was perfect," Ki deadpanned.

Jessie had to laugh. The samurai's humor was rich, but it was also very dry. And just before she fell asleep, she saw a shooting star and hoped it meant that she and Ki would have good fortune on this long journey to California and that Max would be all right when they arrived.

The next day, they rode into El Paso, a city between two low mountains intersected by the Rio Grande River. El Paso was a sun-blasted city of several thousand, and its sister city across the border, Juarez, was even larger. Jessie and Ki had visited El Paso many times over the years, and they rode directly to Mike's Livery, where they always boarded their horses.

Mike Mitchell was in his fifties, big and good natured. He had once been a buffalo hunter but had helped wipe out his own profession. Ten years ago he had bought a run-down livery in the worst part of town, but through hard work and a natural bent for shoeing horses and mules, along with his gregarious nature, he had made himself a successful businessman. Mike bought the best hay and grain that money could buy, and he personally saw to it that every horse ever boarded at his livery left in better condition than it had arrived in.

"Well, well!" Mike shouted, looking up from the hoof he was fitting with a shoe, "if I knowd we was going to have a couple of celebrities ridin' into town, I'd have taken a bath and shaved."

"You're handsome dirty or clean," Jessie said as she dismounted. "How's business?"

"If it was any better, it'd be a real job," Mike said with a broad grin before he turned to spit a stream of chewing tobacco at his forge. The tobacco hit the burning cinders to hiss and steam. It smelled just awful, but then, Mike himself did, too.

"When you gonna marry me, Jessie? I figure between the two of us, we might just make something of that poor old Circle Star Ranch of yourn."

It was Mike's standing joke and one that never failed to make him laugh out loud. And when Mike Mitchell laughed, even the Mexicans in Juárez cringed.

Jessie didn't have the heart to say anything. She knew that Mike expected a look of exasperation and mild outrage, and that's just what she always gave him. But when he'd had his laugh, Jessie gave him Sun's reins.

28

"We're on our way to California," she said.

"What for! You gonna pick them ko-ko nuts along the beach?"

"I'm afraid not. Do you remember our friend Max Maxwell?"

"Sure."

"He's in serious trouble. Something to do with hydraulic mining in the Sierras."

"What's that?"

"They use big hoses to blow down mountains and extract low-grade gold ore."

Mike frowned, and it was obvious that he could not comprehend anyone using a hose to knock down a mountain. "You gotta be . . . funnin' me, Jessie."

"I wish I were," Jessie said. "I've never seen hydraulic mining in action, but I've read about it. They manage to force water off a cliff into a funnel and generate enormous pressure. Enough to wash away tons of dirt every hour."

"Must make a hell of a mud bath," Mike said, no longer grinning, "and I'll bet it messes up things."

"It does." Jessie sighed. "Even worse, it sounds like the family that's behind all of it are ruthless and that Max is on their target list."

Mike scratched a spot behind Sun's ears that made the gelding move closer. "How you gettin' to California?"

"We planned on taking a stage to Tucson and then another to Tonopah and then Reno."

"Stage is leaving in about an hour," Mike said.

Jessie could not hide her dismay. "But it has always departed west on Thursday. That's tomorrow."

"They changed the schedule about a month ago."

"Damn," Jessie whispered, "there goes my feather bed and restaurant dinner tonight."

29

Ki shrugged. He was not a man who took much stock in creature comforts under any circumstances. Even when at the ranch, he slept on a hard surface and seemed to thrive under the most spartan conditions. To Ki, food was a necessity, not a luxury. He was, after all, a samurai, and that meant that he could never allow himself to become self-indulgent or soft.

Mike took Ki's horse also. "When might you be back?"

"I'm hoping before June," Jessie said, quickly untying her bedroll, Winchester and saddlebags stuffed with her personal belongings, which included a fresh change of clothing.

"Well," Mike said, "if you and your friend here ain't back in a year, then I'll just consider these fine horses mine for their board bill."

"If we're not back in a year," Ki said, "we won't ever be needing horses again."

This time, Mike did not laugh.

A short time later, Jessie and Ki were buying tickets to Tucson. The crusty old stage office manager was an ex-driver, and when he looked at Jessie and Ki, he said, "You sure you can't wait and take the next stage west? Next one leaves just one week from today."

"No," Jessie said, "we are on a journey of some urgency. Why do you ask?"

The old man leaned forward and said, "Well, ma'am, it's just that you're a mighty pretty young lady to be ridin' with the likes of the other three passengers that already booked passage on the same stage west."

Jessie followed the man's eyes across the room to see three large and very rough-appearing men slouched near the wall. They were already leering at her with unconcealed lust, and when Jessie looked at them, they grinned.

Jessie glanced at Ki. "They look like real trouble," she said. "I wish we had some alternative."

"But we don't," the samurai said. "So let's just trust that we can handle whatever needs to be handled."

Jessie nodded and turned back to the office manager. "Any Indian trouble between here and Tucson?"

"There's always some Indian trouble," the man said. "But we're runnin' two shotguns on top besides the driver. Last two runs got through without any trouble. Maybe all the Indians figure two good riflemen on the roof are bad news."

"Maybe," Jessie said, not believing it. This particular run had lost many coaches, employees and passengers over the years, but things did seem to be getting better as the army drove the Apache and other raiding Indians either onto the reservations or deep into Mexico.

Jessie paid for their tickets, and as she was about to leave, the old man leaned closer and whispered, "You just be careful with those three. They got the hungry eyes of a lobo wolf, and I figure they're trouble from one end to the other."

"Well be ready for it," Jessie said, looking at Ki and having full confidence that he could handle anyone or anything if she gave him just a little bit of assistance.

"Okay," the manager said, "but I sure wish you would wait just another week."

The old man looked so worried that Jessie patted his hand. "We'll be fine and, if there is Indian trouble waiting for us, those three men look like they'd be able to help put up a fight."

"They sure would, ma'am. Just make sure that it's *Indians* that they're shootin' at instead of you and your friend."

31

★

Chapter 4

When the station master yelled, "All aboard who's goin' aboard for Tucson, Arizona," Jessie and Ki picked up their gear and headed outside.

The three men were waiting. "Ladies first," the largest of the three said, his mouth forming a leer.

Jessie nodded stiffly and started to climb into the coach. Halfway up, however, the big man reached out and patted her rear end.

Jessie started to whirl around and slap the man, but Ki was already in motion. The samurai's right arm blurred as the steel-edge of his hand chopped downward across the big man's wrist.

"Owww!" the man shouted. "Goddamn you . . . "

Again, the samurai's hand flashed, and this time it connected at the trunk of the man's thick neck causing his entire body to shiver like an axed timber and drop.

The other two hard cases were so stunned by the samurai's sudden reprisal that it took them a moment to react. When they did, both men lunged for Ki. The samurai was ready. He ducked under one man's outstretched arms, whirled and delivered a powerful flat-foot kick to the belly that caused his attacker's cheeks to blow out and his eyes to bulge.

"You yellow son of a bitch!" the third man, whose name was Les, cried. "I'll teach you a lesson."

Les's hand streaked for his gun, and it was halfway out of his holster when Ki delivered a perfectly executed *tegatana* blow at the point of his right shoulder, paralyzing the man's entire arm right down to his fingertips. The gun flew out of his hand and he hollered in pain.

The second man jumped back and clawed for his gun, but Jessie's Colt was already aimed at his heart, and she shouted, "Pull it and you're dead, mister!"

The man stared at her and then he lunged at Ki. The samurai started to jump aside but was tripped by one of the fallen men, who yelled, "Get him, Mace! Break his fucking neck!"

Mace was a barrel-chested man who knew the tricks of close-in fighting. He tried to stomp Ki to death but only managed to deliver a glancing blow to the samurai's cheek with the toe of his boot. Ki rolled under the stage and then back out again before Mace could leap on him.

"I'm going to break you in half," Mace hissed.

"You're going to try," Ki said, crouching and waiting for the attack he knew would soon come.

Mace looked at Jessie, who had the other two men covered with her gun. Realizing that he would not get any help, he took a deep breath. "What the hell are you?"

"A samurai."

"A what!"

"Come find out," Ki said with a half smile as he motioned Mace foward.

By now, a crowd had gathered. Some men were actually rooting for Mace because, in their ignorance, they believed Ki was a Chinese, and many were prejudiced against Orientals. Others, like the stage coach manager, however, were shouting for Ki.

34

Ki said, "Mace, it looks like we've got an audience. You want to back down, or get hurt?"

Mace swallowed nervously. Had he not hesitated, he would have rushed in, but now that he had time to think about what the samurai had done to his two friends, both of whom were his size, he was having serious reservations.

"Get him, Mace!" Les screamed. "What the hell are you waiting for!"

Mace balled his fists. He licked his lips, and then he reached for a Bowie knife in his belt.

"Don't," Jessie warned, cocking her pistol.

"It's all right," Ki said, his dark brown eyes never leaving the man's face, "but if you draw that knife, I will break one of your bones."

"Cut him!" Les screamed.

Mace drew his knife, and Ki's hands came up in traditional *te* fighting position, feet apart and positioned for optimum balance, body slightly turned, fingers stiff, shoulders loose and relaxed, eyes trained on the eyes of your opponent so that you begin your move first.

Mace swallowed noisily. He hollered at Jessie. "It's between him and me, lady! You just put that gun away!"

Jessie ignored the demand, knowing full well that if she holstered her gun, the other two men would draw theirs. Men like these had no honor; they asked no quarter and gave none.

Ki danced lightly. "Stage is ready to leave," he said quietly. "Let's not be the cause of it being held up."

Mace forced a laugh. "I never seen a man like you in such an all-fired hurry to be gutted."

They circled each other slowly, oblivious to the shouts of a crowd that grew larger by the moment. Then, suddenly, Mace lunged forward and his blade darted out, but it was a feigned blow designed to test Ki's reactions.

35

Ki, however, did not buy the feigning and stood waiting. Mace said, "You done this before, haven't you, Chinaman?"

"I'm a samurai."

"You're meat!" Mace hissed as he again lunged forward.

Ki rocked back on his heels, and his foot shot out as if it were propelled by some huge steel spring. It went over the thrusting knife and struck Mace in the solar plexus. The man blanched and his momentum carried him forward. Ki spun, and his foot crashed into the man's ribs. Mace screamed and collapsed in the middle as if shot.

Ki dropped down to both feet and decided not to deliver a mortal blow. He knew full well that he had already caved in at least three of Mace's ribs, possibly more. The thug's mouth was wide open, and his face was the color of chalk.

"Finish him!" the stagecoach manager yelled.

But Ki shook his head. The fight was over, and he wanted no part of satisfying the crowd's blood lust. Instead, he simply picked up his saddlebags and gear, heaved them into the coach, then climbed inside and closed the door.

"Hey!" Les cried. "What the hell are you doing! We've got tickets on that stage."

"They've just been punched," Jessie said, her gun trained on the man. "Take the next stage."

"There'll be no stage for you men," the manager pronounced, "I'm refunding your damn money!"

Les's round face went scarlet, and he started to curse, but Jessie did not have to listen to him, as the stagecoach driver cracked his whip and the Concord lurched forward, gathered speed and then rolled out of El Paso in a cloud of dust.

"You were pretty easy on him," Jessie said.

"Too easy, perhaps."

"Why?"

Ki shrugged. "Did you see the children watching?"

Jessie shook her head.

36

Ki gazed out at the sagebrush. "I saw the children watching and there was this one young boy. He had a gentle face, and when I broke Mace's ribs, I could see that he was shocked and a little afraid."

"And that is why you showed the man mercy, even though he had a knife and tried to take your life?"

"Yes," Ki said. "I had beaten my enemy. I did not think it the way of the samurai to humiliate that man. Better I should have killed him."

Jessie nodded with understanding. "I hope that we do not have cause to wish that we had three more guns against the Indians."

"If they come in great force, three more guns would make no difference," Ki said, "and if they do not come, then we will travel easier without them."

"Yes," Jessie said, watching the sun dive toward the western horizon and knowing what the samurai said was always quite logical.

They were to reach a stage station about midnight and have a quick meal and change of horses before continuing. Jessie and Ki dozed fitfully in the coach, their bodies constantly fighting to stay erect and not slide off the leather seats.

"Whoa! Whoa!" the driver yelled to his team, bringing Ki and Jessie awake in the darkness.

"What is it?" Jessie called, poking her head outside the Concord. Then she whispered, "Oh my heavens! Ki, look!"

Ki was already looking out the other side of the coach and also watching the inferno as it sent flames licking high into the night sky.

The driver brought his exhausted team to a halt. Jessie heard one of the guards ask, "What the hell are we going to do now?"

"I don't know," the driver said, climbing down from the box. "That station has the only good water for fifty miles.

These horses ain't fit to turn around and go back without a drink."

Jessie and Ki jumped out of the stage and watched the flames.

"It's *got* to be Indians," the driver said with a sad shake of his head. "I knew the couple that kept that station. They were real nice people. Old man and a woman of about forty. She could cook and he was real hospitable."

"Maybe they're not dead," Jessie said. "Perhaps they escaped before their station was fired."

"Not very damn likely," one of the guards said.

"But possible," Jessie argued.

"It's more likely that the Indians are still camped thereabouts someplace and just layin' for us," the driver said.

"Well, what are we going to do?" the younger of the shotgun guards demanded in a high, nervous voice. "We can't just sit here worrying all night."

"I will go and see what awaits," Ki said.

"You what?"

"I am *ninja*," Ki explained. "I can go and return without being seen."

"The hell you say!" the guard swore. "The Indians can do that in the dark, but I never heard of nobody else that could see in the night."

Ki did not bother to explain again. Instead, he ducked inside the coach and, in a few minutes, emerged in his *ninja* costume, which could best be described as a form-fitting black suit like a coverall, with a hood that covered Ki's head except for a narrow eye slit.

"What the devil you going to do in that getup!" the driver demanded.

Ki ignored the stupid question and said to Jessie, "I will return within one hour."

"Be careful."

Ki nodded and reached back into the coach for his bow and quiver of arrows.

"What the hell!" the driver swore. "You'd damn sure better be armed with a gun and a rifle!"

Ki did not listen to the man. He used the ancient samurai weapons exclusively, and they always served him very well.

"That's the damndest shaped bow I ever saw," a guard said.

Ki had heard that comment a hundred times before. The samurai bow was oddly shaped to a Westerner. It was light-colored and made of layered strips of wood, glued together and wound at several critical points with red silken thread. The bow's core was sandwiched between two pieces of bamboo, which had been tempered by a special fire treatment, giving the weapon an unusual amount of strength and flexibility. Developed over the centuries, the samurai's bow might look odd to an Indian or a frontiersman, but it could fire arrows with amazing speed and power. Additionally, the bow's sharpened tip and its rough gut string were excellent weapons.

The driver shook his head. "Boys," he said, "after the way I saw this fella handle them three cutthroats back in El Paso, I just got a hunch that he knows what he's doin' no matter how odd it looks to us."

Ki appreciated the driver's wisdom. It showed him to be of more than average intelligence.

"Ki," Jessie said, "just promise that you'll come back for help if there are more than a couple of them. There is no sense in taking chances."

"I understand."

Satisfied that his bow and arrows were ready, Ki slipped into the brush, suddenly *ninja*. As he moved toward the burning station, he well remembered how Hirata had taught

39

him to think about using every feature of the topography, no matter even if he were sneaking across an open courtyard. He was always to train his eyes to see even the smallest of things that would be useful as cover, to find the shadows and to move like one of them until he had completed his mission of secrecy and often of death.

Yes, he thought, gliding through the brush, low and silent, I am *ninja* now, the invisible assassin of the Japans.

★

Chapter 5

When Ki drew nearer to the burning stage stop, he could see the shadows moving about on the opposite side of the fire and knew that they were caused by either horses or men. Circling around the inferno, Ki crept through the sage until he arrived at the edge of a large clearing, then he flattened to the earth and saw three Indians rummaging through broken boxes and crates of supplies and food, which they had apparently pulled from the station before applying their torches.

Off to one side, Ki saw the bodies of five white people and a dog. The samurai remained motionless, wanting to be very certain that there were no more Indians off somewhere in the brush.

His patience was rewarded a few minutes later when he saw two more Indians emerge from the brush, dragging what appeared to be a very battered and half-naked young woman. Ki thought that she must be dead, and if she wasn't, then she was no doubt wishing to be. The Indians would have raped her repeatedly, and if they had not already killed her, the woman would suffer and die in the next few days.

The Indians had discovered and already consumed several bottles of whiskey. Now, they pitched the woman to the

41

ground and joined their friends in searching for more whiskey. It was obvious to Ki that they were slightly drunk.

As Ki watched, the Indians grew more and more upset because they could not find additional bottles of whiskey. Finally, one of the Indians grabbed the young woman by the hair and twisted her head back so that her features were reflected in the flames. The drunken warrior shouted in the young woman's face, and then he snatched up one of the empty bottles and held it to the firelight. He pretended to drink.

Ki did not hear the young woman's cry, but he saw her bruised mouth open and the gleam of wet tears on her cheeks. When the warrior twisted her hair even harder, the woman tried to bite and claw, but the Indian smacked her with the bottle and drew his knife.

Ki knew that he had to act or the young hostage would be dead before he could return with Jessie and the stagecoach employees. Reaching over his shoulder, his fingers located Death Song, an arrow that bore a small ceramic bulb just behind the arrowhead. Death Song had, for centuries, been used by samurai to drive terror into the hearts of their enemies. As the arrow flew toward its mark, air would pass through a hole in the ceramic bulb and cause Death Song to screech eerily, the sound ending suddenly when the arrow ripped through its fleshy target. Almost always, Death Song demoralized a samurai's opponents.

"Kill me!" the woman screamed as she managed to rake the warrior's cheek. "Go ahead and do it!"

The Indian seemed to understand and with blood welling on his face, he was more than willing to satisfy the white woman's plea.

But Death Song was already nocked on Ki's bowstring, which Ki drew back to his ear. When the samurai fired, the bow turned 180 degrees, and Death Song began its screaming journey through the darkness. The Indians froze with a look of bewilderment on their faces, and then terror when the shriek ended with the warrior clutching his chest and the arrow.

Before the Indians could do anything, Ki was already fitting a second arrow and firing it at the nearest warrior, who took the arrow in the throat and went down kicking and screaming. Ki jumped forward, and his hand reached inside his black *ninja* costume. He moved so swiftly and blended so well with the shadows of darkness that another Indian died from one of his *shuriken* star blades before any of them could react, half-drunk as they were.

Ki pulled his favorite weapon, which was the ancient and dreaded *nunchaku*. Ki's half-sized version was called the *han-kei*, and it was nothing more than two perfectly fitted sticks of heavy wood attached to each other by a short length of braided horsehair. The sticks were only seven inches long, but as Ki whirled one of them, while holding the other, it made an ominous whirring sound until it smashed into the side of a warrior, crushing his skull. Another warrior foolishly tried to block the weapon's path with his forearm and paid the price with broken bones.

The last Indian standing seemed to realize he was doomed, and yet, he screamed and threw himself forward. The *han-kei* choked his scream into silence.

The samurai turned away from the warriors, allowing the one with the broken arm to escape with his life as Ki rushed to the side of the young woman.

She was dazed, and when he knelt by her side, she recoiled in terror. Ki pulled off his black hood.

"I will not hurt you," Ki said, removing his *ninja* tunic and slipping it over the girl's shoulders to hide her ravaged body. "You are safe now."

"Who are you?" she whispered, her eyes filling with

wonder as she gazed at his glistening body bathed in the firelight.

"That is not important," he said, thinking of how she must have been very pretty before the Indians had misused her.

Suddenly, the woman threw herself against Ki's chest and began to sob hysterically. Ki held her close and waited, knowing that Jessie and the others must have heard Death Song, that Jessie would know that there was a fight and would come running.

Jessie and the others did arrive a few minutes later, and when they counted four dead Indians among the dead whites, they were amazed.

"You did this?" the driver whispered in a voice filled with awe.

"I had to," Ki said. "They were about to kill this young lady."

The three men stared at her and then looked away quickly for it was easy to see what the girl had suffered.

Jessie went to her side. "Let me help you."

But the young woman steadfastly refused to let go of the samurai. Finally, Ki had to unlock her hands from around his neck, and then he said in a very gentle voice, "This is my best friend, Miss Jessica Starbuck. She can help you now better than I can. You can trust her."

The girl stared into Ki's face for a long moment, and then she nodded and Jessie took her over to the well. "Will one of you draw me some water?"

One of the shotgun guards hurried to help as Ki climbed to his feet, then extracted his arrows and the *shuriken* blade from his victims while the other two stagecoach employees watched.

"A warrior got away," Ki said. "I do not know if he will be able to reach his tribe soon and bring more to avenge the death of these men."

The driver was the first to snap out of his reverie. "I guess that means we ought to water the horses and ourselves real good and then turn around and head back to El Paso."

"No," Ki said. "We must push on to Tucson. It is a matter of life or death."

"You sure as hell got that right," the older of the two guards said. "*Our* lives or deaths!"

"We have no more reason to believe there is trouble ahead than behind us," Ki reasoned. "The Indians could be any-where out here—or hundreds of miles away."

The driver scowled and scrubbed his face. "I just don't know," he said. "I'm gonna have to think on this some. Ain't worth losin' our lives to make this run to Arizona."

Ki decided to say no more. He would back whatever Jessie wanted to do, and he was sure that she would want to continue on toward California.

"We ought to bury the dead," Ki said, beginning to search for a shovel.

"I ain't burying no damned redskin," the guard swore. "Not after what they did to these people and to that poor girl!"

Ki figured that the Indians would rather not be buried anyway. The important thing, he reasoned, was to bury the whites, get the horses watered and then put as many miles between them and this place as they could.

"How far is the next stage stop?" he asked.

"About a hundred miles. I ain't sure that the team we got now can made it that far without grain."

"They have to make it," Ki said as he searched for a shovel to do the burying.

Burying the dead had not proved an easy task. They had finally located two shovels, but their handles were burnt away, and because the Indians had tossed debris down the

45

well, getting enough water for the horses and everyone, plus filling the stagecoach's desert water barrel, had taken the rest of the night.

The girl's name was Linda, and three of the dead were her mother, father and young husband. The other two remaining corpses were the station tender and his wife, the woman who could cook so well.

As sunrise raced across the hard land, Jessie again said a few words over fresh graves, while Linda sobbed uncontrollably and the three stagecoach employees stood with grim and worried expressions, with their hats in one hand and rifles in the other.

"Amen," Jessie said, ending her prayer for the souls of the departed.

Linda had to be pulled away from the graves and then gently helped into the stage.

"Do you have other family?" Jessie asked her.

"No. They were all I had. I'm alone now."

Jessie and Ki exchanged concerned glances. Jessie said, "We are going to California, but I think you'd be much better off remaining in Tucson."

"*If* we arrive," the younger guard, whose name was Vincent, said.

Jessie shot the man a hard and disapproving glance before turning back to the girl. "I can find people to care for you in Tucson. I have some friends there, and I'm sure. . . . "

"No!" Linda reached out and clasped Ki's hand.

The samurai shifted uncomfortably. "Jessie is just trying to do what she thinks would be best for you."

"I need to stay with you."

When she said that, she was staring right into the samurai's eyes.

"All right," Jessie said. "You can remain with us just as long as you choose."

Linda visibly relaxed. "I don't know what I'm going to do now," she said. "I loved Roy, and now. . . . "

"You're still very young," Jessie said. "I know that you probably can't imagine a life without your family and husband, but there will come a day when you will marry again."

Linda gave no reply and Jessie did not press the matter. She was not sure of the girl's mental state but certainly understanding of her hardship. "We have to go."

"I found some grain and fed the team," the stagecoach driver said. "It was spilled all over the place, but it wasn't hard to scoop up. Musta been fifty pounds of barley, and the horses ate it like candy. It'll do them a lot of good."

"I'm glad to hear that," Jessie said. "By the time they're replaced, they'll have pulled this big stage a long, long ways."

"At least we hope so," the driver said.

Ki helped both Jessie and Linda into the coach, then climbed in after them and shut the door.

A moment later the coach was again rolling westward, but Jessie was no longer sitting beside Ki, because the young widow would not let loose the samurai's strong right arm.

★

Chapter 6

By the time the stage Jessie and Ki were riding approached the next station, they were surrounded by the giant saguaro cactus in Arizona Territory. Linda had made a remarkable recovery. She was fortunate to be Jessie's size and could, therefore, wear the extra dress Jessie had packed before leaving Circle Star. With her hair combed and her skin freshly scrubbed, she did not even remotely resemble the poor woman that they'd rescued from the Indians.

Only the faint bluish bruises around her eyes and her mouth gave visible evidence to the terrifying ordeal that she had survived, thanks to the samurai. Yet Jessie could see that there was a deep sadness within the young woman, and she often observed Linda's face in unguarded moments when her eyes grew misty with a faraway look that said she was remembering her late husband and parents.

"Only time can heal the deep losses," Jessie told their new companion. "I lost both my parents, and still the emptiness of their passing remains. However, the pain is no longer sharp, and the bitterness I felt at the injustice of losing them has been replaced by acceptance and happy memories."

"What about you, Ki?" Linda asked. "You've never said anything about yourself."

"I don't remember my father. He was an American sailor who died shortly after I was conceived. My mother is only a dim memory."

"But there must be someone."

Ki nodded, and because he liked and trusted the young woman, he told her about Hirata.

"That is a beautiful story," she said. "I just wish that it had not ended so tragically."

"Oh, but it was not tragic," Ki told her. "Hirata died well."

"But he *killed himself*."

"Yes," Ki admitted, "he did that. Yet it was as he wished and according to his beliefs."

"Would you . . . "

"No," Jessie said before Ki could formulate an answer to the single question he had never quite resolved. "Ki is my friend. As long as we live, we will protect and help each other."

It was clear from the confused expression on Linda's face that she did not understand this at all. She had been wondering almost from the start what exactly the relationship was between the handsome half-Oriental fighter and the beautiful woman he accompanied.

"Listen," Jessie said, "Ki and I are . . . how shall I put this?"

"Of one spirit," the samurai suggested, "but not of one body."

Jessie's eyebrows arched. "That is a very apt description, Ki. Thank you!"

"You are welcome."

Linda could not hide her shock. "Then you mean you don't . . . "

"No," Jessie said with a shy smile. "We don't."

"Oh."

50

There was an uneasy silence between them for the next few minutes, and so when the stage driver shouted from up above, Jessie was greatly relieved.

"The station is still standing!" the driver called down to Jessie, Ki and Linda. "No sign of trouble."

Jessie poked her head outside and, about a mile ahead, saw a rock-faced dugout, several corrals, a well, and a small shed that was cluttered with wheels and blacksmithing tools. When a burly man with a long beard stepped out of the dugout and hailed them, Jessie relaxed.

"They've got fresh horses," Jessie said. "It's a good thing, because our poor El Paso team is about to drop. And at the rate we've been traveling, it would take a month to get to Reno."

"Let's just hope that we can get out of this Apache country and that the Paiutes up in Nevada are at peace."

"Paiutes?" Linda asked. "Are they also unfriendly?"

"They have been known to fight," Jessie said. "In fact, they actually shut down the Pony Express some years ago. It seems that one of their women was violated and they wanted justice."

Linda's eyes dropped to her hands in her lap. "I had never thought about the fact that we might also violate their women."

Jessie could have bitten her tongue off for bringing up the subject. "I'm sorry," she said, "it was thoughtless of me to bring up a subject that would cause you pain."

"No," Linda said, "I remember reading that it is not healthy to block things from your mind. That will drive you crazy. But in truth, after my parents and Roy were killed, I remember very little."

Ki reached over and placed his hands on those of the woman. "You are a strong person, Linda. I know that you will find happiness again some day."

She looked up at him suddenly. "I owe you so much that . . ."

Ki shook his head. "Let us not speak of that again. We must get ready to eat. Are you ladies hungry?"

Both Jessie and Linda nodded, and their somber mood changed as the stage rolled into the Arizona station and they were hailed by the station tender.

Even before they disembarked, the driver and his guards began telling the bearded station tender all about how the last station had been burned to the ground and how the tender, his wife and Linda's poor family had been killed.

"But that samurai," the driver said, pointing to Ki as he helped Linda and Jessie to the ground, "he shore did even things up. Killed five of them all by himself!"

"Four," one of the guards said. "He only killed four."

"Four or five, what the hell difference does it make!" the driver snapped. "Any way you look at it, there was a hell of a lot of Indians and that funny dressin' fella killed 'em all by himself."

The station tender was a heavyset six-footer with large arms and a barrel chest. He had a habit of constantly picking at his long salt-and-pepper colored beard.

Pulling it as he swaggered over to Ki, he sized the samurai up and said, "Hard to believe a man no bigger than you could do all they say you did."

"Now, Bull, you just let him be," the driver said. "I wouldn't have believed it myself if he hadn't whipped three big old boys just before we left El Paso."

The station master wanted to try Ki on for size because he was much the larger man, but when he looked into the samurai's eyes and saw no fear or even concern, he backed down.

"I don't half believe what they're telling me," he said, "but I'm here to help passengers, not stir them up."

"Then perhaps you had better go inside and cook us a meal," Ki said. "Because we're all hungry and it's been a long, long road."

Bull blushed with anger before he wheeled around and marched back into the dugout.

"Never mind him," the driver said, "he's always been a hard-nosed bastard. They say he was once a bare-knuckles fighter and a champion, too. But of course, that's his story. All I know is that if you look at his knuckles, you can see that every one of them has been broken in a fight, and he didn't get that squashed nose from shoveling horseshit."

"Some men," Ki said, "have always got to prove something to themselves. I pity such men because when they grow old, they'll have nothing inside to hold valuable."

The younger guard, Vincent, frowned. "You sure are a strange one the way you fight and act. Are you any good with a Colt or a Winchester?"

Ki almost smiled because, out in the West, these were the weapons that men were measured by. "I can shoot both with considerable accuracy," he said, "but I am not as skilled as a professional gunman."

"I guess you don't need to be, given how you can kick and shoot that crazy bow of yours."

Ki said nothing and followed Jessie inside the dugout, where a handsome but very shy Mexican woman in her mid-twenties was busily frying beans, tortillas and chunks of beef and peppers. The food smelled wonderful, and when they all sat down before their plates at a long table, the woman quickly began to dish it out.

"Conchita cooks the best Mex food in the whole damn Southwest," Bull boasted. "I bought her off some Apaches who stole her from down in Mexico someplace. She tried to run away a few times, but I figure I got her broke to stay now."

"Exactly what does that mean?" Jessie asked in a cold voice.

"Well, ma'am," Bull explained, "it's like this. The way you train a dog to come when it runs is to keep a long leather string around its neck. If you call the dog and it don't come quick, you jerk the string so that the dog sorta chokes up. Only takes a couple times of that sort of thing before the dog begins to understand that it's gonna be in pain if it don't obey its master."

"Conchita is not a dog," Jessie said. "She's a human being, and if she wants to return to Mexico and her village, you should not only let her go, you should take her there."

Bull bit into a thick roll of tortillas and chuckled as he chewed. "Lady," he said, "if I let her go, I'd have to do all the cooking, and the nights would be real lonely. Know what I mean?"

The man laughed at the color that crept into Jessie's cheeks. He laughed so hard he got to coughing and spitting food.

Ki was about to say something when Vincent, the young guard, exploded in anger. He had had a difficult time keeping his eyes off Conchita, and now he shoved back from the table and came to his feet.

"It's like Miss Jessica said, that girl ain't no damn animal, and you got no right to keep her here if she wants to go back home!"

Bull stopped laughing and coughing. He also came to his feet, and now he reached out to grab young Vincent by the shirtfront and haul him across the table. But the stagecoach guard jumped back and said, "You want a piece of me, Mister, you step outside so we don't ruin the ladies' dinner."

"Well then, let's just do 'er!" Bull roared.

Jessie started to object. Vincent was not a big man and

certainly no match for the veteran bare-knuckles fighter. But Vincent was too angry to be reasonable, and as he headed for the door, he stopped beside Conchita.

"When I finish with him, you can go on with us to Tucson," he told the Mexican woman. "You understand any English at all?"

"*Sí*, but you should not do thees. He will kill you!"

"No he won't," Vincent promised. "So pack your things, Miss."

Conchita's dark eyes moved from one man to the next. "Please," she told the driver, "you must stop thees!"

"Too late," Bull said, gesturing at Vincent. "Come along, boy, I'm about to take you to the woodshed for a whippin' you'll never forget."

"Ki," Jessie said, forcing herself to remain seated, "would you please see that Vincent is not maimed or badly hurt?"

The samurai nodded and followed the other men out the door. In the yard, Vincent and Bull squared off, each spitting on his knuckles and circling warily. Vincent threw the first punch, and to Ki's way of thinking, it was a good one. The young guard was very fast, and Bull was far too slow to get out of the way. The station tender rocked back on his heels, and before he could recover, Vincent came in swinging from every angle.

Ki saw at least four of the much lighter man's blows land against Bull's face and chest before the station tender, with one mighty haymaker, knocked Vincent flat on his back.

Bull laughed, wiped a smear of blood from his lips and sneered, "Get up! I ain't about to let you quit until you've had a good lesson in how to speak to your betters."

Vincent staggered to his feet, wobbly-legged. "You ain't my better," he said, "you're just a big, overgrown . . . "

Bull charged and even though the young guard tried to get out of the way, his legs were too wobbly, and so Bull's shoulder hit him in the chest and knocked him end over end. Bull grabbed Vincent by the shirtfont and hauled him to his feet. He cocked back his fist, but Vincent still had some fight in him, and he drove his knee into Bull's groin.

The big man's mouth formed a large circle, and he released Vincent and grabbed for his balls. Vincent landed two more punches, and then he stood back and shook his head while Bull groaned and tried to recover.

"Don't give him any time to come back," Ki warned. "He's hurt, so finish him before he recovers and finishes you."

Vincent took the samurai's advice. He went after Bull with both hands, and even though his punches lacked great authority, his fists were a blur and each one left a bright red mark on Bull's face.

Ki thought for sure that Bull was going to fall, but he saved himself by grabbing a hitching post, and then, with his back turned to Vincent, he lashed out with his boot and caught the younger man in the belly, doubling him up.

Bull, his face crimson with blood, swung around and kicked Vincent again, this time in the knee. Ki heard the knee pop and then Vincent screamed in agony. Bull wiped his bloody nose, laced his fingers together and hammered Vincent like a nail. The young man was finished, but Bull wasn't. With Vincent helpless on the ground, Bull reared back with his boot and aimed for Vincent's head.

The powerful station tender would have killed Vincent had the toe of his heavy boot collided with the younger man's temple. Ki did not let that happen. Taking three quick steps, he jumped forward and his right foot caught Bull squarely in the face. The man bellowed in pain and staggered.

"Look out!" the driver yelled as Bull tore his six-gun from his holster.

Ki's hand streaked for his *shuriken*, but Vincent's own gun was in his fist and bucking with smoke and lead. Bull took three faltering steps back and then he crashed over and lay still.

Conchita, Jessie and Linda had watched the fight from the doorway, and now the Mexican woman came racing across the yard to throw herself down beside Vincent and hug his neck.

"*Muy gracias! Muy gracias*," she kept repeating as she helped Vincent get up on his one good leg.

Ki went to the young man's aid. "Let's get you inside and I'll take a look at that. Maybe it's just dislocated and I can set it right again."

Vincent's face was bloodless and his teeth were clenched with pain. "Will I hang?"

"No," Ki said. "Any jury would call it self-defense."

They brought Vincent inside and sat him in a chair. Ki's hands slipped up and down the man's knee, and when he was sure that it was a dislocation, he threw one of his legs over Vincent's leg, placed both his hands on the side of the knee and said to the driver and the other guard, "Pull straight when I give the word."

The driver started to object. "But . . . "

"Just do as he says," Les, the older guard, snapped. "He's done everything so far he's set out to do, hasn't he?"

The driver nodded and took a hold of Vincent's toe while Les grabbed the ankle. Being a samurai, Ki was more knowledgeable than most doctors in the subject of human anatomy. He had learned from old Hirata every pressure point and every bone and joint. He knew where an opponent was the most vulnerable, and he knew exactly how much force to use depending on whether he wanted to kill, maim or simply disable his opponent.

Now, he took Vincent's knee between his strong brown

hands, and his fingers locked over the dislocation and judged exactly how to correct it.

"Pull!"

When they pulled, Ki forced the joint back into its socket, but before he could tell them to stop pulling, both he and Vincent were dragged to the floor.

"What happened to him!" Linda cried.

"Santa Maria, ees he dead!" Conchita shrieked, dropping to Vincent's side.

Ki climbed back to his feet. "He's not dead. He just fainted. When he comes around, he'll be just fine, but it will take a week or so before he can move very well. He's probably torn some ligaments, and that knee is going to be pretty painful."

The driver shook his head. "Well, what are we supposed to do? It's still a ways to Tucson."

Ki shrugged. As far as he was concerned, he had done his part.

Jessie expelled a deep breath. "The team we brought in is exhausted, so they can't go on behind our coach. I think the only solution is to leave Vincent. When the next stage arrives, he can either ride it to Tucson or stay on and work this station."

"Sure," the driver said. "The company is sure going to need someone here. Conchita, will you stay with him until he can travel?"

The Mexican girl nodded and hugged Vincent's head to her large breasts. "He ees very brave. Muy hombre, eh!"

"Yes, he is," Jessie said, suppressing a grin.

Les shook his head. "That lucky sucker is going to be real slow healing unless I'm mistaken. I'll bet it takes him a good month or longer before he gets out of bed."

"You're just mad that you didn't stand up for Conchita so's you could stay here a few weeks."

"You damn sure got that figured about right," Les growled. "Can we sit down and finish eatin' before any other damn thing happens?"

"That's a good idea," Jessie said.

A few minutes later, Vincent had regained consciousness, and when he heard the plan about his having to remain at the station, he could hardly contain his joy at this piece of good news.

"Don't you worry," he promised, "me and Conchita will hold things down real well here. In fact, we might even want to stay—but if Conchita wants to return to Mexico, I reckon I'll have to take her down to her village."

"It would be the right thing to do," Jessie said, "but somehow, I think she'll be happier here with you."

"We'd better bury old Bull before we leave," the driver carped. "I still ain't sure how I'm going to explain this to the company."

"Just tell them," Jessie said, pursing her lips thoughtfully, "just tell them that accidents do happen."

"Yeah," the driver said, "that and a nickle will just about get me a cup of coffee and a termination notice when we arrive in Tucson."

★

Chapter 7

Tucson was one of Jessie's favorite high-desert towns, and she knew from her history lessons that it had originally been founded by the Spanish explorers and missionaries as the presidio of San Augustine de Tucson one hundred years earlier. Although it had been frequently attacked and overrun by the fierce Apache, the town had survived. Now, located on the east bank of the Santa Cruz River, the town had air that sparkled, and because of its higher altitude, the summers there were much more charitable than in the lower deserts.

Besides farming, Tucson had experienced a mining boom when gold and silver had been discovered in the valley. The Sorora Exploring and Mining Company had employed hundreds of men, and when its mining operations began to flag, new ore discoveries had been made in nearby Bisbee and Tombstone. Not many years earlier, Tucson had been designated the territorial capital.

When the stagecoach rolled into town, Jessie wasted no time in finding out when and where she could switch to another stage traveling northwest to Tonopah and then on to Reno.

"There wasn't one leaving until next week," she said when she returned to Ki and Linda. "And since we can't wait that long, I hired Les away from his company and bought a serviceable spring wagon and pair of wagon horses."

"That might be a little hard on Linda," Ki said.

"I think not. The wagon has two well-cushioned seats, and I am having the blacksmith reinforce and add new springs so that the ride will be almost as comfortable as a Concord. You see, the wagon was once used by a drummer, but the sides were taken off so that only the top remains. At least that way we will be out of the sun, and the wagon is light enough for fast travel."

"It sounds perfect," Linda said.

"I hope so." Jessie frowned. "I also purchased a thirty-gallon water barrel, several extra rifles and a second pair of horses in case the first pair should falter or go lame."

Linda was a little overwhelmed by Jessie's expenditures and preparations, but Ki wasn't. It was typical of Jessie to simply buy whatever was necessary to accomplish her goals.

"We'll be leaving the first thing in the morning," she said, "and we all have rooms at the Drover's Hotel."

When they arrived at the elegant Drover's with its landmark crystal chandelier hanging over the lobby, Les said, "Miss Starbuck, do you suppose I could have a little advance on my salary?"

"What about your guard's pay?"

"Well, leavin' the company sudden like made 'em pretty testy. They stalled me on my back pay. Said it wouldn't be ready for a few days, and of course, we'll be long gone by then."

"Very well," Jessie said, digging into her pockets and paying the man ten dollars. "Just make sure that that our wagon and horses are outside and ready to travel at first light."

"I will, ma'am." Les thumbed back his hat. "But I guess you know that we'll have to keep buying fresh horses all along the way. Even though you have a pair of extras, judging from the hurry you're in, we're gonna need more animals."

"We'll find them," Jessie said, already thinking about tomorrow's journey. "Ki, we're going to need food, the usual extra supplies and grain for the horses."

"Is your wagon large enough to hold everything?"

"Yes. I'm even having the blacksmith nail a box on the back that can be locked and which will contain a sheet of heavy-gauge metal."

"What for?" Les asked.

"To deflect bullets or arrows from the rear," Jessie said. "Just in case."

Their new driver was quite obviously impressed by Jessie's foresight. "You sure don't miss much, do you?"

"I can't afford to miss a thing," Jessie said. "Mistakes out in this country, as I'm sure you are well aware, are generally fatal."

That night, they all ate in the hotel's elegant dining room and had a meal fit for a king, with plenty of good French wine and strawberry shortcake for dessert.

Jessie excused herself and went to bed early, Les headed for whatever pleasures he sought, and that left Ki and Linda to themselves.

"I had better be going to bed, too," Ki said. "It's a long way to Tonopah, and it's hard country. There's no telling what kind of difficulties we might run into."

Linda paled a little. "You're referring to Indians, aren't you."

It was not a question, and Ki had no intention of lying to the girl. "The Paiutes, as I've explained, have been known to attack isolated travelers. But frankly, there are quite a few renegades and misfits out on the roads looking for easy pickings."

"We're not easy at all," Linda said. "I mean, you alone are capable of. . . . "

"Yes," Ki interrupted, "but then I had the advantage of

63

being sober and catching those five Indians by surprise. Had it been daylight and their minds clear, I'm afraid things might have worked out much differently."

Linda swallowed. "I just wish that we could stay here in Tucson for a while and rest."

Ki took her arm and led her up the hallway to her room. "You can stay and rest, Linda. Jessie and I suggested that very thing several times. She would pay your room for as long as you thought you'd want to stay and give you—"

"No," Linda said, "I couldn't do that. I'd want to earn my own way. In fact, I am hoping that I might find some way to repay you and Miss Starbuck for your kindness and for saving my life."

"No payment is expected or required." Ki held out his hand. "Give me your key and I'll open your door."

She gave him the key, and when her hand touched his, Ki saw that she shivered. "Are you all right?"

"Oh yes," she said quickly. "It's just that, well, there is something about you that makes my mind whirl. I can't explain it. Around you I feel all mixed up."

Ki suppressed a smile. "Then go to bed. You've been through a lot, and it's a credit to your strength and resilience that you're doing so well."

"It is?"

Ki opened the door. "Yes," he said, stepping back so that she could pass.

But Linda did not move. "Would you like to come stay with me awhile?" she asked, unable to meet the samurai's gaze.

"I don't think so."

Now she looked up at him. "But why? Is it because you know what the Apache did to me?"

"Of course not."

"Then. . . . "

"I just don't think you're quite ready for this," Ki said. He leaned over and kissed her on the forehead, and then he turned and walked toward his own room.

"Ki?"

He stopped and turned around. "Yes?"

"When you do think I'm ready, will you make sure and let me know?"

He chuckled. "You'll be the first and only one to know. Good night, Linda."

"Good night," she said, shaking her head with wonder as she closed her door.

The next morning when Ki, Linda and Jessie left their hotel for the spring wagon, they had a rude shock because not only was it missing but so was Les. Ten minutes later, they were standing in the sheriff's office, grim-faced.

"Your friend got drunk and wound up in a poker game in one of the worst saloons in town. Got himself killed before the night was over."

"Killed?" Jessie asked.

"That's right. He was playing faro with some *banditos*, and when the cards started runnin' against him, he called the Mexicans cheats. When the gun smoke cleared, the *banditos* were standing and your friend was left on the floor in a pool of his own blood."

"Damn," Jessie swore, shaking her head. "Well, I guess we'll just have to go on without him."

"What about the burial?" the sheriff asked. "Somebody needs to pay for it."

"Let the El Paso Coach and Freight Company pay for it out of Les's overdue wages," Jessie said with exasperation. "I'm already out money."

Jessie was steaming when they arrived at the blacksmith shop and livery where she'd bought the spring-wagon and had it worked on the evening before. Unfortunately, there was more bad news.

"Those Mexicans over there say that the wagon and the four horses you bought from me yesterday now belong to them."

"What!"

"That's what they say. I think you'd better go for the sheriff. They look pretty determined."

"Well so am I," Jessie said, marching over to three Mexicans, who sat watching the wagon and horses with hard expressions.

Jessie spoke fluent Spanish, and she wasted no time in telling the three men that the wagon and horses belonged to her.

The largest of the three lit a cigarillo and shook his head. "They belong to us," he said in Spanish. "We win them last night at cards."

"They weren't yours to win," Ki said, "so you'd best just ride out and count yourselves fortunate that you're not in jail for murder."

"We may be yet if you interfere," the Mexican said, smoke curling up to make his eyes squint. "Who are you, Chinaman?"

"I'm her friend," Ki said, taking the measure of the trio and thinking that he would be able to get two of them but probably not three. These were very hard men and dangerous from the looks of them. They'd be called *pistoleros* in Mexico, *banditos* north of the border.

"And so am I," Linda said, snatching an old double-barreled shotgun that had been propped up just inside the livery's door.

Linda cocked back the hammers on the old weapon and pointed it right at the three Mexicans. "*Adiós*, señors!"

No one had paid any attention to the young woman until

this instant, but when the three Mexicans saw the shotgun trembling in Linda's hands, they grew very nervous.

"Don't shoot us, señorita," the leader said.

"I will shoot you if you don't ride off and leave us alone!"

The Mexican knew that he was beaten. Up until then, he had been cocksure that he and his two *compadres* could easily kill Jessie and Ki. But now that he was staring down the barrels of that big rifle, he had a change of heart.

"You are very brave, señorita. Perhaps we will have the pleasure of meeting again. My name is Manuel Lopez de Villa Escobar Ramos."

"I don't care what your name is," Linda said, the shotgun dancing crazily in her tiring arms as she held it up. "Manuel, you and your two creepy-looking friends just ride on out of here!"

The Mexican smiled, and he was actually handsome except that two of his front teeth were missing. "You are plenty of woman! I like that! Not as pretty as your friend, but. . . . "

"Get out of here," Ki said, weary of listening.

The Mexican's grin faded and he glared at Ki. "I think we will see each other sometime out there on the long trail, eh, señor?"

"You'd better hope not."

Ramos and his two unsavory friends spurred away, leaving Ki, Jessie and Linda in their dust.

"You are a brave woman," Jessie said, taking the shotgun from Linda's hands.

"She's crazy as hell is what she is!" the liveryman swore. "That Ramos is one of the most dangerous men in the whole Southwest on *both* sides of the border. And he's not likely to forget your shamin' him that way."

"He shamed himself," Ki said, "and if he comes after us, he won't live to do it a second time."

"Talk is cheap," the liveryman said. "The three of you are no match against them."

"That," Jessie said, "is where you are most definitely wrong."

She smiled at Linda. "You should be very proud of what you did just now. It took plenty of courage."

"I just saw the rifle setting over there and grabbed it," Linda admitted, now that she had begun to shake in a delayed reaction. "If I'd have had time to think, I might not have done a thing."

"Yes, you would have," Jessie said. "You've got spunk and courage. And to be real honest about it, you're probably going to be far more valuable to us than Les ever could have been."

Linda's eyes widened with happiness. "Do you mean it!"

"Of course! You just saved our lives, didn't you?"

"Well, no! I mean, Ki would have done something to them. I probably saved *their* lives."

Ki smiled. "You are too modest. Anyway, thank you."

Linda blushed under their praises. Already, she felt as if her spirit was being reborn and that she would useful to her new friends.

"Is the wagon finished?"

"Yes, ma'am," the liveryman and blacksmith said. "I put the steel plate in the back and the box is just as you wanted."

Jessie inspected the work. It was not pretty, but it would do as she intended and give them an element of safety in case they were attacked.

"Let's hitch up the team, tie the spare horses to the back, finish loading this thing and get out of here," she said.

Ki and Linda nodded and set to work, both of them all business and very much aware of the trouble that might await them along the hard miles yet to be traveled.

★
Chapter 8

After the three Mexican *banditos* were driven off, they went straight to their horses. Ramos, his blood fired by humiliation, tightened his cinch and then inspected his pistol.

"We will be waiting for them at Picacho Peak," he said to his two friends. "And there, we will ambush and kill the Chinaman and then capture the women."

"For ourselves first, and then for Charro," one of the Mexicans said.

Ramos nodded. "We must make sure that the women are good, eh?"

The other two *banditos* laughed coarsely. "Charro will pay well for them. Especially the one with the big breasts, red hair and all the money."

"Yes," Ramos said, "but it is the other one that I want most. That woman would have killed me."

"Many women would like to kill you," the man named Juan snickered.

"It is true," Ramos said, a little proud of the fact. "Antonio, what do you think of them?"

Antonio was the quiet one of the three. His lean, hawkish face was knife-scarred, and he was missing one ear and two fingers from his battles. His disfiguring scars and his skill with a knife gave him great pride, and there were women below the border who thought him very handsome and brave.

"I think," Antonio said, "I want them both."

"Yes," Ramos said after a minute, "we will all have them both. But which one do you want first?"

"The rich one," Antonio said, remembering Jessie's flashing green eyes and long, shapely legs.

"Then so be it! Juan, you will have whichever one we finish with first."

"That will be the short one, because you fuck like a chicken, so fast!"

It was a joke, and they all laughed, though Ramos's manhood was slightly offended. "Let's ride!"

As the three Mexicans left Tucson at a hard gallop, Jessie, Ki and Linda finished loading and hitching the wagon. When the extra pair of horses were securely tied behind the wagon and the water barrel was fastened in place, their preparations for the long journey to Reno were finally complete.

"Let's go," Jessie said, climbing up into the front seat and taking the lines as Linda and Ki also took their places.

The liveryman shook his head with resignation. "I think you're crazy goin' off in that thing," he said. "If Indians don't get you, them Mexicans damn sure will."

"We appreciate your warning," Jessie said as she slapped the lines and the horses propelled the wagon forward.

Jessie had been driving buggies and wagons since she was a girl, and now she skillfully weaved her way though the busy streets but stopped at Peterson's Mercantile on the west end of town and handed the lines to Ki, saying, "I'll be right back."

"Can I help?" Linda called.

"No. I just need to make a quick purchase. I'll be back in a few minutes."

Linda twisted back around on her seat. "What do you think she is going to buy in there? She's already bought everything I could possibly think of for this trip."

"Whatever it is," Ki said, "you can bet it's important. Miss Starbuck doesn't do anything without putting some thought into it first."

A few minutes later, Jessie hurried back out and handed a heavy sack up to Ki saying, "A little surprise for any unexpected company we might have."

Ki opened the bag and pulled out a couple of sticks of dynamite. "Nice," he said.

"Do you know how to use them?" Linda asked in a nervous voice.

"We sure do," Jessie said, climbing back up into the wagon and taking the reins from her friend. "And there are times when a few well-placed sticks of dynamite can be almost as effective as the United States Cavalry."

Ki replaced the sticks of dynamite and set them carefully down between his legs, but Linda remained apprehensive.

"Are you sure they'll be safe there? I mean, all the bouncing around and everything. . . . "

"Won't detonate them, I promise," Ki said. "The only real danger might be if they are hit by a stray bullet. Now that would cause quite a bang."

Linda paled a little. "Then, why. . . . "

"If that happened," Jessie explained matter-of-factly, "we'd be blown to smithereens quicker than you could blink your eye, and so there'd be no reason to worry."

Linda clamped her mouth shut, but she did not look at all convinced that the reasoning of her companions was sound.

Picacho Peak, a huge pile of volcanic rock rising several hundred feet above a cactus-strewn valley, was about fifty miles northwest of Tucson and had always been a landmark for travelers, much like Chimney and Independence Rocks along the Oregon Trail.

Pima, Papago and Apache had used the sweet springs that bubbled out from the base of the peak to quench their desert thirsts for centuries. Later, Spanish missionaries on their brave forays to Christianize the Indians had stopped at Picacho, and when the Mormon Battalions built the first roads across the southwest in 1846, they also took comfort in the shade of the peak and in its delicious waters.

Four years later the Butterfield Overland Stage Line kept a station at the pass, but it had most recently been destroyed by the Indians. And finally, Picacho Peak had the dubious distinction of being the westernmost battleground fought between Union and Confederate soldiers in the spring of 1862.

When Jessie pulled their weary team up toward the distant peak, she said, "We won't reach it before midnight, but I don't see that we dare stop out here. There's no water."

Ki and Linda were in agreement. The day had been warm, the water holes few and far between. Already, the thirty-gallon water barrel was three-quarters empty.

"Then let's push on," Ki said.

Linda nodded in agreement. They had been on the road almost ten straight hours, and her backside was numb, her spine ached and even her neck was stiff from the jolting. She would not have complained for the world to Jessie, but the blacksmith in Tucson had done a poor job on the springs and this wagon was not nearly as comfortable as a Concord stage.

Jessie drove on into the night. The road leading toward the dark, silhouetted peak was broad and in surprisingly good condition. There were places where the wind had cut hard ripples so that it was as bumpy as a washboard, but other than that, they had made good time.

"If those Mexicans are waiting for us," she said, sometime after ten o'clock, when they were still about five miles distant from the peak, "then I think this would be the natural place for an ambush."

"I agree," Ki said. "I think it would be wise if I became *ninja* and went on ahead. Besides, I need the exercise."

Jessie understood and approved of the samurai's decision. Back at Circle Star, hardly a day passed that the samurai did not run for many miles so that he was always in top condition. For a such a man, sitting all day was especially tedious and uncomfortable.

In the semidarkness under a golden wedge of moon, Ki quickly changed into his *ninja* costume. He then took his bow and arrows and prepared to leave.

"Why don't you take a stick of this?" Jessie asked, reaching into the sack and pulling out dynamite, then tossing it to the samurai.

"It is not a samurai's weapon."

"I know that, but it's bound to be pretty effective. Besides, you said yourself this afternoon that you needed to make some new arrows."

Ki grudgingly admitted that this was true before turning to leave.

"Wait," Jessie called, "what about matches?"

"I will not need them," Ki said, turning back.

Linda was confused. "But how can you. . . ."

The samurai vanished into the brush and rocks before Linda could phrase her question, so Jessie explained. "If there are enemies waiting for us, Ki will pitch the stick of dynamite in their campfire, and it will explode, no matter how small the fire. And if there are no enemies, then he will return with the dynamite and we will make camp for the night."

"I see," Linda mused aloud. "You and Ki seem to be

able to read each other's minds. How?"

"We have been very close since my father's assassination. After a while, you sort of get to know what the other is thinking. It is easier for me to follow Ki's thinking because it is so logical. But when he attempts to second-guess me, he has more of a problem."

Linda smiled, but then her brow furrowed. "Don't you ever wish that you and he could . . . well, know each other as man and woman?"

Jessie was glad that it was dark enough that the girl could not see that her cheeks were growing red. "I do," she admitted. "I suspect that Ki is a wonderful lover. In fact, I have had women tell me so."

"He has had many women, I suppose."

"Yes, he has. Ki is a very attractive man, as I'm sure you've noticed."

"I sure have," Linda said. "Whenever I think about it, I feel ashamed, though, because Roy only died a little while ago."

"Don't be ashamed or torment yourself with guilt," Jessie told her. "What you feel is very natural."

Jessie waited a few minutes more, and then she shook her reins and the wagon rolled forward. "Would you reach behind you and grab my Winchester?"

"Do you really expect trouble up there?"

"I don't know," Jessie said, "but it always pays to be ready."

Linda handed Jessie her rifle, and then she took one of the extras and laid it across her own lap, saying, "I don't even know how to tell if this thing is loaded."

"It's loaded," Jessie said, "and all you have to do if we are attacked is to aim and fire, then lever in a fresh shell, aim and fire again."

"I'll never hit anything."

"Most often," Jessie said, "just being under fire is enough to scare an ambusher out from his cover, and that would be a big help."

Linda studied Jessie's profile in the moonlight. "You know, I almost get the feeling that you and Ki enjoy danger."

Jessie smiled. "If it seems that way, maybe there's at least an element of truth there. I know one thing—Ki and I both detest boredom and routine. I think that's why we're such a good match."

Linda looked away because, given how traumatic her life had been as of late, she welcomed the thought of safety and routine. Her poor Roy had been the son of a farmer, and she and her husband had been on their way to New Mexico Territory, where they'd heard there was still good farmland to be homesteaded. Roy had been steady and gentle. Linda knew she could have set her watch by the regularity of his daily routines. Funny, then, Linda thought, why does the samurai, who is my Roy's opposite, have such appeal to me?

Linda could not answer that question beyond the obvious fact that Ki had saved her life and was very strong and handsome. But in temperament, he was quite unlike her late husband.

When the samurai crept near the small campfire on the far side of Picacho Peak, he flattened on the earth and remained motionless for nearly ten minutes before he was certain that two of the *banditos* were missing, while the one that remained watched their horses.

That much determined with certainty, Ki moved without further delay. He slipped and slithered through the rocks and brush until he was only a couple of yards from the Mexican; then, he gathered himself and jumped forward.

One of the horses saw the sudden movement and reared

back in fright. The Mexican, sensing danger, frantically grabbed for his pistol, but the steel-hard edge of Ki's hand struck his wrist, and the Mexican's hand went dead.

The Mexican snarled and filled his lungs to shout a warning to his friends, but Ki's foot caught him in the throat and the warning was strangled into silence. Unfortunately, however, the horses broke from their pickets and thundered off into the night.

"Juan!" the familiar voice of Ramos hissed. "What the hell is going on down there!"

"*Nada*," Ki hissed back as he began moving swiftly toward the voice, which he judged to be some fifty yards up the side of the peak.

"But the horses!"

Ki forgot about using the dynamite and instead drew a *shuriken* star blade. When the form of Ramos jumped up and was silhouetted against the skyline, Ki hurled the blade. It glinted in the moonlight, and when it struck Ramos in the forehead, the man screamed, batted at his head and then crashed over in the brush, kicking in death.

Antonio was no place to be seen, but Ki knew the tall, thin *bandito* was close. He searched frantically for the man during the next five minutes, and because of the poor light and the fact that the mountainside was so rocky, he could not find any tracks.

For an instant, Ki was frozen with indecision, and then he turned and sprinted for the road, hoping to intercept Antonio before the man could reach Jessie and Linda.

But a few minutes later, he skidded to a halt, seeing that he was too late. Antonio had managed to slip up behind the two women, leap onto the wagon and put his gun to Jessie's head. Now, as Ki stood in the road, he could see that the *bandito* was grinning in the moonlight.

"Come visit us," Antonio said.

76

When Ki did not move, Antonio cocked his pistol and spat, "I count to three, and then this woman's brains will feed the lizards tomorrow, señor!"

"Ki," Jessie whispered, "don't listen to him!"

Ki did listen, and when Antonio reached the count of two, the samurai moved quickly forward. "What do you want?"

"Your life, hombre," Antonio said. "Turn around."

"No!" Linda cried.

"Turn around or these women are dead!"

Ki started to turn, and as he did, he heard a cry of pain. He ducked as a bullet exploded overhead, and he felt a searing pain explode across the back of his eyes. Ki hit the dirt, rolled as another bullet bit into the road, then looked up to see that Jessie and Linda had both grabbed the *bandito*'s right arm and were trying to tear his pistol away.

Ki tried to jump to his feet, but he was dizzy and so grabbed the nearest wagon wheel and pulled himself erect. When the pistol exploded harmlessly into the wagon bed, Ki yanked his *tanto* blade from its sheath and buried it into Antonio's lower leg.

"Ahhh!" the *bandito* cried as the gun finally jumped from his hand.

Antonio reached for his knife, but it was too late. Jessie's own six-gun was already leaping from her holster, and it bucked in her fist twice. Antonio threw his head back, so that his eyes were on the moon, and he howled in death.

When the man crashed headfirst off the wagon, he knocked Ki down and the samurai lost consciousness. Thinking he could hear his name being called, he struggled desperately to reply, but his lips would not move and his tongue was thick and unresponsive.

Jessie was at his side a moment later, and so was Linda.

"He took a bullet across the scalp," Jessie said, pulling

77

the samurai's blood-soaked hood back.

"What are we going to do!"

"We'd better get him into the wagon and up to one of the springs, where we can make camp and doctor that wound. If he's suffered brain damage, we'll know soon enough."

Ki, hearing Jessie's voice, struggled up from darkness like a man who had dived too deep into cold, dangerous water. But at last, his head surfaced, he gulped fresh air and his eyes opened to see the faces of two beautiful young women.

"I'm not brain damaged," he said between gritted teeth.

With squeals of joy, both women hugged him almost to the point of suffocation. Ki struggled a little but he had to admit that suffocating between the bosoms of Jessie and Linda would be a very nice way to die.

Chapter 9

Ki recovered, and fortunately the long road that took them across the muddy Colorado and up through Tonopah, Genoa, Carson City and finally to Reno was tiring but blessedly uneventful.

Reno had been nothing before the discovery of the fabulous Comstock Lode, but nearby Virginia City had changed all that. Overnight, tens of thousands of would-be gold seekers dashed over the Sierras from the played-out California gold country. They streamed through Reno on their way to the great underground mines.

Reno became a shipping center, a bustling center of commerce. Every day, huge shipments of supplies and machinery passed through Reno on the way to the Comstock. Ten years later, when even the Comstock fortunes had began to lag, the Central Pacific Railroad had slammed over Donner Pass and laid rails through Reno, making it the major distribution center for hundreds of miles around.

Now, with the Truckee River, which flowed through the city, almost overflowing its banks with spring run from the Sierra snowpack, Jessie, Ki and Linda arrived at the Overland and were greeted by the manager with a wide smile.

"Miss Jessica Starbuck! What a pleasure to have you stay

with us again! And you, Ki, we are always honored by your Oriental presence."

"Thank you," Ki said rather formally as the man grabbed his hand and worked it up and down like a water pump.

The manager, whose name was Clinton Seabrook, beamed at Ki and Jessie before his discerning gaze settled on Linda. One look told him that she was not high society. Her clothes quite obviously belonged to Jessie, and her fingernails were chipped and probably had never been manicured. Her hair, while a full and rich brunette, appeared dull and uncombed. No question about it, she was quite ordinary indeed.

Seabrook tried to hide his note of disapproval because Linda was definitely not up to the standards of his hotel and clientele. "Mr. Seabrook at your service," he said coolly, and then he turned away before Linda could think of a reply.

Ki and Jessie both noted the man's snobbishness, and Jessie said, "Mr. Seabrook, this is Miss Linda Washington, great great granddaughter of our first president. She is considering buying some of my ranches and holdings. I hope you will give her the best service available. Who knows, she might even be interested in purchasing this hotel."

Linda blinked, Ki remained stoic, but Seabrook almost swallowed his tongue. He stared, and then his mouth opened and closed twice before he bowed as if he had been cut in half. "Miss Washington, what an honor to have you as our guest!"

Linda was momentarily at a loss for words, but recovering quickly, she said, "I am delighted to be here. Tell me, what value do you place on this establishment?"

"Value?"

"Yes."

"Well, I really don't know." Seabrook adjusted his tie. "I . . . I suppose that it might be worth . . . oh, fifty or sixty thousand. It is, after all, the finest hotel in Reno."

"Which isn't saying much, is it," Linda mused aloud, and she turned a full circle as if inspecting every nook and cranny. "I see much that needs to be changed."

When she uttered that last remark, her eyes came to rest on Clinton Seabrook, and she studied him as if he were a laboratory specimen.

Seabrook colored, and his eyes searched Jessie's face, begging for help. But Jessie let the man squirm. After all, his initial manner had been highly insulting and he needed a hard lesson.

Visibly sweating, Seabrook stammered, "Miss Starbuck, we have important documents and material forwarded from your San Francisco office."

Linda cleared her throat. "Mr. Seabrook, do you know the location of Pineville?"

Seabrook mopped his brow. "Why . . . that might be down south below Carson City."

"It's in California," Linda said coldly.

"Oh, yes! Of course! I recollect that now. But as to the exact location, well, porter!"

A weary-looking porter in a red uniform shuffled over with a bored expression on his face. "Sir?"

"Miss Washington would like to know the exact location of Pineville, California. I seem to have forgotten exactly where that fair town is. Can you help us?"

"Sure. It's about fifty miles south of Hangtown."

"Isn't that called Placerville now?" Jessie asked.

The porter nodded. "It sure is, Miss Starbuck. Best thing to do is to board the train that leaves every morning. You'll go up the mountain, over Donner Pass and then down to Hangtown. Get off there, and you can hire a cab or a wagon to take you the rest of the way down to Pineville."

"Is it a nice town?" Jessie asked.

"Once it was."

"*Was?*"

"Until the Power Mining Company moved in with all that hydraulic mining they do. I understand that now folks are deserting like rats off a sinking ship. It's a shame, Miss Starbuck. It was a real nice little community. Passed through it a time or two. It was the kind of place this town used to be before the arrival of the Central Pacific. Back then it was called Lake's Crossing and—"

"That will be all, Herbert," Seabrook said in an icy tone of dismissal.

Herbert nodded, rolled his eyes and shuffled back to his station beside the hotel desk while his manager steamed.

"It's impossible to hire decent, respectful help these days," Seabrook said carpingly.

Jessie and Linda had decided to share a suite, and Ki would have one adjacent to theirs. Before Herbert left them alone, Jessie tipped the man handsomely and said, "I'll want dinner brought to this room along with those documents that were sent over from my San Francisco office."

"Yes, ma'am," Herbert said. As he started to leave, he turned and stared at Linda.

"Is something wrong?" she asked.

"Oh, no! I was wondering if I could have your autograph. I read all about your great great grandfather. President Washington was one of the greatest men who ever lived."

Linda shot a worried look to Jessie, who said, "I'm sure Miss Washington would be flattered to give you her autograph."

"Yes. Yes, I would," Linda said lightly before she took the outstretched pen and paper that Herbert was extending.

After she signed, Herbert was very pleased, far more so than he had been even after he received Jessie's magnanimous tip. And just before he closed the door on his way out, he said, "I hope that you do buy this hotel, Miss Washington, and that the first thing you do as owner is fire Mr. Seabrook. He's a real idiot!"

Jessie and Linda both burst out laughing as the door closed quickly behind the disgruntled porter.

"Imagine," Jessie said, "me being someone important like you said!"

Jessie's smile faded. "You *are* important," she explained, suddenly quite serious. "Back in El Paso you might have saved our lives."

Linda thought about that for a moment. "Hmm," she mused aloud, "if that were true, I *would* be important."

"It is true and you are very important. I have a feeling that you are going to be a great help to us when we reach Pineville."

"But how?"

"I don't know. It's just a hunch, but my hunches are usually correct," Jessie said as she marched straight for the bathroom and a bath that was already filled with hot soapy water. After traveling hundreds of hard, dusty miles, it was a well-deserved luxury she could afford.

★

Chapter 10

After Ki and Linda went out for dinner, Jessie finished her bath, then dined alone in her room, perfectly content to relax in the solitude of her own company. About eight o'clock that evening, she finally got around to opening the large packet she had requested from her San Francisco office manager, Bill Fellows.

Opening the packet, Jessie extracted a letter and read it out loud. "Dear Miss Starbuck. Enclosed you will find the information you requested both on hydraulic mining in the West as well as the Tower family and their mining company, currently operating in Pineville and points south. As you can soon tell, the Tower family are universally hated and utterly ruthless when it comes to the extraction of low-grade ore bodies found throughout the Sierras. I have enclosed several articles and photographs that graphically show the absolute devastation caused by hydraulic mining, of which the Tower family are the recognized authorities. The utter destruction shown in these pictures make them almost hard to believe, yet I am told that it is even worse than we can imagine."

There were a few more paragraphs from Fellows concerning other matters relating to business, but Jessie paid them no attention once her eyes focused on the pictures and the articles about hydraulic mining.

What Jessie saw were pictures of entire mountainsides being eaten away by immense and incredibly powerful jets of water forced out of nozzles under enormous pressure.

Jessie stared at the pictures for several minutes, her anger and outrage building. At last, she began to read the enclosed articles on the Tower family and their immoral practice of raping the Sierra countryside. She was at least a little encouraged to discover that two of the five articles—and the ones most vehemently opposing hydraulic mining—were written by Max Maxwell, her old friend.

Jessie put the pictures and articles aside just after midnight and went to bed. She had learned that the head of the family responsible for so much carnage was named Gordon Tower, and he was the part of a very wealthy industrial family from Massachusetts. Apparently, Tower had brought his wife to San Francisco almost thirty years before, during the California Gold Rush. Like thousands of other argonauts, Tower had raced to the diggings and then jumped from one strike to the next without ever really finding much gold.

Desperate, half-starved, discouraged, and with his wife pregnant and sick, Tower had disappeared for about a week and then triumphantly returned with a saddlebag of gold nuggets, claiming that he'd "struck it rich" in a glory hole.

But his wife was already too weak to deliver what turned out to be twin boys. She died in a long and difficult childbirth. Tower never forgave himself for leaving his wife, and he also blamed the Sierras for his tragic loss. About a hundred miles north, two dead prospectors had been found, and many folks believed that Tower had killed them for their pokes, but no proof of this was ever found. Eventually, Tower used his gold nuggets to buy other claims and a few dry goods stores. He prospered, went into dredging and redirecting entire streams and rivers, then hit upon the method of hydraulic mining.

Today, Tower was one of the wealthiest men in California, and his twins, Jason and Aaron, who were now only a few years older than Jessie, were the heirs apparent to the Tower holdings. To Jessie's way of thinking, the entire saga of Gordon Tower could have and should have been an American success story except that it seemed fairly obvious that the man had murdered two innocent prospectors to get his stake. And once he'd gotten it, he'd let nothing stop him from becoming rich and seeking vengeance against the mountains he blamed for his wife's untimely death.

Jessie turned out her light and went to bed with a troubled mind. She supposed that Ki and Linda were in bed, too, probably just the thickness of her wall away. Well, so be it, she thought. Their need for each other has been growing every day, and this had to happen sooner or later. Better tonight than later, when they might be up to their eyeballs in trouble over near Pineville.

Besides, Jessie thought as she drifted off to sleep, a man or a woman can think more clearly when their physical needs aren't so dominating.

Alone in his room at last with Linda, Ki wasted no more words. He knew that she wanted him so badly that she was almost feverish, and he wanted her with the same powerful intensity. Standing beside his bed with the window open to bathe them in moonlight, Ki worked the buttons of her dress free, and each one that loosened caused her to tremble with expectancy. When the buttons were finally all free, the young woman wiggled her body and the dress fell to the floor around her ankles. Now, she stood in the moonlight wearing only a pair of knee-length pantalettes, her nice, firm breasts quickly rising and falling for his inspection.

Cupping her breasts, she whispered shyly, "They aren't nearly as big as Jessie's, I'm sure, but they ache for you."

"As I ache for them," the samurai said, lowering his head so that his lips brushed her hard nipples.

Linda's head rolled back on her shoulders, and she sighed with pleasure as her hands slipped down and unbuttoned Ki's trousers. Reaching inside them, she whispered, "This is what *I* want."

"You will have it," he promised, "all of it."

"Mmmm," she murmured, "and it is very large."

Ki had not been with a woman for weeks, and he quickly stiffened with desire as Linda's fingers expertly stroked his shaft into its full hardness. Linda pushed herself back and slipped out of her pantalettes. Then she smiled and raised her hands over her head and did a little pirouette that caused the samurai to smile.

"If you feel like dancing just now, then go ahead," he told her. "It will be my great pleasure to watch."

She laughed and lowered her hands. "I have always loved to dance, but right now, all I want to do is make love with you."

Ki finished undressing and moved up against her. She took his manhood and rubbed it against her most sensitive place while he again kissed her breasts. Linda moaned softly and rolled her shoulders back and forth to make sure her breasts received Ki's equal attentions. And then, arching her back, she parted her legs slightly and tucked Ki's throbbing sword between her pale, quivering thighs. Then she grabbed his buttocks and pulled him hard inside of her.

"Oh," she breathed, "you fill me completely."

"Why don't we get on the bed?"

But Linda didn't seem to hear him as, standing on her toes, she began to bump hard against him. Ki chuckled and backed her up against the wall, then began moving in and out of her with long, slow but very deep strokes.

Linda hopped up, and her legs locked around the samurai's narrow waist. She kissed him, her tongue going into his mouth and her heart pounding against his chest as their bodies moved with increasing tempo.

"This is better than anything I'd even imagined," she moaned. "But hurry! I feel like I'm going to explode!"

Ki's lips pulled back from his teeth, and he thrust at her harder and harder until she threw her head back and cried out with pleasure. Ki felt her insides milking him wildly, and then his knees buckled for an instant and his legs shook as he filled her with torrents of his hot seed.

"Oh my," she was finally able to gasp as he waddled over to the bed and fell on her. "Dear Roy was good, but you were wonderful!"

Ki smiled down at her. "I hope you want more because it's going to take most of the night for me to get enough of you."

Linda nodded eagerly. "Give it to me all you want, darling. I don't think I could ever get enough of you."

Ki's mouth found her breasts again, and before long, he could feel a sweet ecstasy building deep in his powerful loins.

"Here it comes again," he panted, thrusting wildly into the moaning woman beneath him. "Here it comes!"

Linda cried out, too, and her strong little body, slick with sweat and their love juices, took all the samurai had to give.

When Jessie awoke, it was very early and she was not surprised to see that Linda hadn't returned to the room. Jessie smiled a little wistfully, remembering how her walls had shaken last night as the pair had coupled only a few feet away.

Dressing quickly and taking a quick review of the materials that had so disturbed her the night before, Jessie left her room and went downstairs to have breakfast.

"I trust you slept well last night," Clinton Seabrook said brightly.

"I did after all the shaking finally stopped."

The hotel manager's eyebrows shot up quizzically. "Shaking, Miss Starbuck?"

"Yes, shaking."

"But I felt nothing, and none of the other guests felt an earthquake in the night."

"Who said anything about an earthquake?"

Jessie left the man to ponder in confusion. A short time later, she was joined by her samurai, and she said, "I've taken the liberty of ordering your usual breakfast. I trust that you worked up a good appetite last night?"

Ki blushed, and for one of the rare times, he was actually stumped for words. "I . . . I apologize," he said finally, grabbing his water glass and drinking it in great gulps.

"Apology accepted," Jessie said with a half smile. "Just next time you make love to a woman, do it in bed or at least against the *far* wall."

Greatly desirous of changing the subject, Ki said, "Last night before dinner, Linda and I walked over to the railroad depot. The train for Sacramento leaves at nine o'clock sharp."

"Then we had better eat, pack and be on our way within the next hour," Jessie said, "although the transcontinental railroad is rarely on schedule."

"Just our luck it would be this morning."

Jessie studied the samurai over her steaming cup of coffee as she waited for their breakfast to be served. "You look a little tired this morning, Ki. Tonight, in your own best interests, it might be prudent to have Linda stay with me."

"Yes," Ki said, speaking to his empty plate. "I think you are right."

"We are up against three Tower men, not one," Jessie told the samurai. "I saw a picture of them in a clipping from the *Sacramento Bee*. They are all cut from the same rough block."

"How old are the sons?"

"They are twins and only a few years older than ourselves." Jessie reached into her pocket and produced the clipping. "Here are their pictures so that you will know them the instant they are first seen."

Ki studied the picture, which, although it was not of high quality, was still good enough to allow him to recognize the bull-shouldered, square-jawed and very ornery-looking family of men.

"They don't like like the kind who will be very reasonable."

"I agree," Jessie said as their breakfast arrived, "but then, if they were reasonable, Max would never have pleaded for us to come and help save his life."

★

Chapter 11

The Central Pacific Railroad was two hours late, but then, so were most of the passengers who boarded for California. Before going to the depot, Jessie had sold her modified spring wagon and four good horses, the proceeds to be distributed to a home for the aged.

Once they were on the train, it puffed out of Reno, climbing almost from the start. Ten or fifteen miles west of town, it began to climb in earnest as it followed the surging Truckee River up toward Donner Summit. Jessie and Ki had been over this rail many times, but not Linda, and the scenery as they slowly churned up the eastern slope of the Sierras was spectacular.

"It is so beautiful!" Linda exclaimed, looking back toward the broad Nevada high desert country. "I never imagined it was such a wonderful sight."

"It wasn't very wonderful for Crocker and his Chinese who built this roadbed and all these huge snowsheds that we're about to pass under," Jessie said.

A moment later, they did pass under a snowshed that was nearly half a mile long.

"My gosh!" Linda said. "It must have taken a forest just to build those things."

"Almost," Jessie said, "you see, the Central Pacific tried everything to keep these tracks clear of snow during winter, but nothing worked. Five locomotives all hooked together behind a twenty-foot-high snowplow could not break through the drifts and aftermath of almost continuous avalanches. Finally, they built these snowsheds with a steeply sloping roof so that the snow slides off and down over the side of the mountain. It's the only thing that would work."

"Didn't the Chinese build most of this?"

"That's right," Ki said. "There were some Irish and other nationalities, but the Chinese were the only ones willing to brave the deep snows, avalanches, freezing weather and thin air. They finally had to use nitroglycerine to blast under Donner Summit because the rock was so hard and the tunnels required were so long. Dynamite wouldn't do the job."

"And," Jessie said, "there was a race going on between them and their rival, the Union Pacific, driving westward from Omaha, Nebraska."

Linda shook her head. "All I remember from my schooling is that the two railroads met somewhere in Utah Territory."

"Promontory Point," Jessie said. "Someday the Southern Pacific or some other railroad will similarly link the Southwest, perhaps from Texas to Los Angeles. But no one is holding their breath."

"Look," Ki said, pointing out the left window just to the south. "That's Donner Lake."

Linda nodded. "It's beautiful. Is that where the Donner Party was stranded?"

"No," Jessie said, "they were caught just this side of the summit. We'll pass very close to the site. There are some wooden crosses that you'll see."

"How many perished?" Linda asked quietly.

Jessie paused for a minute to think. "Let's see. I seem to recall that of eighty-nine who left Fort Bridger in the summer of 1846, only about half lived to reach California. The rest died of starvation or exposure to the cold. They were victims of a very early snowfall and one of the worst winters in memory. Up here, the snowpack can get more than thirty feet deep."

Linda sighed. "Those poor people. Isn't that the way life is sometimes? I mean, it seems like good or ill fortune plays such a large part in success or failure."

"Maybe," Ki said, "but I seem to recall that the Donner Party was plagued by bickering and bad thinking almost from their formation. One of the party even stabbed to death another and was banished somewhere out in the Nevada desert."

"You're at least partly right, though," Jessie said to the young woman. "Sometimes life goes against you no matter how hard you prepare and how much you work to meet every possible complication. And other times, for example, Ki and I have just been damned lucky we weren't killed."

They lapsed into silence and continued slowly up the mountain, three locomotives straining and billowing thick black smoke from their fire stacks as they labored higher and higher.

"Over there," Jessie said, pointing with a grim expression. "Do you see the crosses?"

Linda nodded. "They're so big. And what are those ax cuts on the sides of the trees marked with ribbons for?"

"That's to mark the depth of the snow when the Donner Party was found."

Linda shook her head. The marks on the pines were a good forty feet off the ground. She could not imagine snow ever becoming so deep.

"No wonder they were trapped," she whispered. "Does the snow get this deep in Pineville?"

"I doubt it," Ki said. "Hangtown is much farther down the western slope, and if Pineville is at about the same elevation, then the snow won't be nearly as deep."

"I hope not."

Jessie smiled. "Why, Linda, are you planning to remain here?"

"No. But you never can say for certain."

"That's true." The samurai nodded with agreement. "Look, here come the tunnels."

There were three Summit Tunnels under Donner Summit, and the westernmost one was the longest, almost a quarter of a mile long. The train plunged into total darkness, and as the heavy smoke from its fire stacks filled the tunnel, Jessie felt her eyes sting and she could hear passengers coughing.

At last, they burst back into daylight, traveled only a few minutes and entered and exited tunnels twice more.

"Are we done with them?" Linda asked, her eyes weeping.

"Yes," Jessie said, "but now you can see why black powder and dynamite proved so worthless in tunneling. It caused so much smoke that it would take half a day for the tunnels to clear out so that the Chinese coolies could return and work. Nitroglycerine, I'm told, not only was about ten times more powerful, but it left very little smoke and so the tunneling could proceed much, much faster."

After rolling through the tunnels under Donner Summit, the train slowly picked up speed and then began to brake as it started its descent down the western slope of the Sierras. It stopped at several little towns, including Dutch Flat, and then Jessie remembered that Hangtown was actually south of the railroad.

"I'm afraid we'd better get off at Cisco, which is coming up next."

Ki and Linda grabbed their belongings, and when the train stopped, it was for no more than three minutes, as passengers hurriedly disembarked as well as boarded. Jessie hailed one of the wagon drivers that were always hoping for passengers.

"We need to reach Pineville," she said to the dusty man, who sat chewing on the stem of a corncob pipe.

"Well that's nigh-on seventy mile or more," the man said. "Damned if I'm agoin' *that* far!"

Jessie had no patience with contrary men, but since there appeared to be no other drivers waiting to earn a fare, she said, "Listen. How about taking us as far as Hangtown?"

"Why, that's a day ride there and another back!"

"Twenty-five dollars," Jessie said. "That's a month's pay for a lot of men."

The driver sucked wetly on his pipe for a minute, and then he said, "Chinaman gotta ride along with you ladies?"

"The hell with it," Jessie said, picking up her bags. "We can find someone else to deliver us to Hangtown."

"All right! All right!" the driver shouted, jumping from the seat of his wagon and grabbing the bags from Jessie and Linda's hands. "I never said I wouldn't take the Chinaman. I just asked if he was going along for the ride, and now I can see that he is. We'll get along fine."

Ki could not entirely hide the fact that he was miffed. "We will if you keep your mouth shut and your eyes on the road."

The driver didn't like that. He clamped his teeth down hard enough to make the bowl of his pipe lift an inch, and then he snorted, "Hmph!"

Jessie didn't like the man, but she could not afford to be choosy, so she climbed up into the driver's seat and Linda came up beside her. Ki, however, was more than happy to hop up on the wagon bed and dangle his feet over the back.

"Let's go," Jessie said, noting that the man's two bay mares were as sorry and unenthusiastic-looking as their owner.

The ride down to Hangtown was long, but at least the scenery was more interesting than the desert they'd already crossed. Jessie, Ki and Linda all insisted they stop for a short rest at the little village of Coloma, which was the site of the discovery of gold by John Marshal. Nestled on the south fork of the American River, there was nothing that remained of Sutter's original sawmill, but it didn't take a great deal of imagination to visualize how it must have been more than thirty years earlier, when Marshal accidently discovered big nuggets of gold in the mill race. It was a discovery that would bring tens of thousands of argonauts rushing to California from all over the world and, ultimately, destroy Marshal and even John Sutter.

"They was fools the both of them," the driver said. "They should have just kept their mouths shut, panned the gold as long as they could and walked away millionaires. But they had big mouths, and soon, everyone was rushin' in here aclawin' and ascrapin' for gold. Both men wound up paupers. Marshal became a drunken sot, and Sutter lost every damn thing he owned."

Jessie could not hide her irritation. "Yes, they made plenty of mistakes, but I don't see how anyone could have kept the discovery a secret for very long. After all, there were men crawling all over this country by then, and it was just a matter of time before someone made the discovery."

The driver shook his head with disagreement. "If it'd been me, by gawd, I'd have done it different, and today I'd be as rich as a king and a sight happier than I am now."

"We'd better push on," Jessie said. "It'll be dark before we reach Hangtown."

"Ain't that what I been telling you all along?"

Jessie curbed her anger, and when they finally did arrive that evening, she paid the man without comment, and they found comfortable accommodations for the night.

The next morning, she went directly to the livery and bought a buggy and a nice carriage horse.

"You sure must be in a hurry," the liveryman said, pocketing Jessie's cash with a wide smile. "Why, there's a mail wagon that goes down to Pineville and points south every day. You could have ridden it for a dollar each."

"No thanks," Jessie said. "I'm fed up with hiring fools and complainers to drive us. From now on, we drive ourselves. How far is it to Pineville?"

"Twenty miles. Maybe a few more. You can't miss the turnoff to Pineville that goes east and climbs up the mountains about five miles."

"Big sign?"

"No," the liveryman said, "big damned mud slide caused by hydraulic mining. They've completely fouled up the South Fork of the Cosumnes River."

"The Tower Mining Company?"

"Yeah. How did you know?"

"I just had a hunch," Jessie said before she drove away, dreading what she expected to find twenty miles ahead.

★

Chapter 12

The liveryman who'd sold Jessie the buggy and horse had not been exaggerating when he'd described the mud pile that had once been a mountain. Jessie, Ki and Linda stared with disbelief at the carnage that had taken place. Instead of rocks and mountains, there was a five-square-mile area of nothing but twisted layers of dried and cracked mud. An entire forest had been knocked flat by the hydraulics, causing trees to lie twisted like bones crusted with mud.

The destruction was so complete that, at the instant it was first witnessed, one's mind refused to believe one's eyes.

"Oh my God," Jessie whispered. "I can't believe it."

"Believe it," Ki said quietly.

Linda simply shook her head and averted her eyes. "It looks like an infected, running sore."

Jessie thought that was a very apt description, given that the mud-filled river sort of seeped and weeped its way through the devastation. "I guess we might as well go on to Pineville," she said, turning the wagon up toward the higher mountains.

Two miles over the ridge, they were back in forest again, but they could see and hear men working on giant flumes that would bring an entire river down through their nozzles.

Now Jessie could see why the water pressure was so amazingly powerful.

"Look up there," Ki said, pointing to a cluster of white tents, where a large and busy work camp was obviously being used as a base of operation. "Tower Mining Company."

Jessie had to squint her pretty green eyes to read the sign painted on one of the tents, but she was able to read the faint lettering.

"We'll be paying them a visit before much longer, I can tell you that much," she said angrily.

"We can," Ki said, "but from the size of this operation, I can see why Max needed our help. This Tower family has a small fortune tied up in hydraulic mining."

"That tells me they're making a large fortune," Jessie said.

"So what are we supposed to do?" Linda asked. "Even you aren't rich enough to buy up the entire western slope of the Sierras."

"Don't be too sure of that," Ki said.

"Bosh!" Jessie slapped her lines sharply against their horse, which jumped forward and continued on up the road toward Pineville.

When they first saw the little mining and logging town, they were immediately taken with its charm and beauty. Unlike most of the gold rush towns that had mushroomed, then withered and died in a matter of weeks or months, Pineville was situated on a nice river and there were many small farms surrounding it, along with a few moderate-sized cattle and horse ranches.

"It's still pretty," Jessie said as they rounded a bend in the road, banged over an old wooden bridge that forded the river and entered on the town's main street.

They saw several saloons, a small Wells Fargo office, a bank and several stores that seemed to advertise in their windows everything from licorice to Doc Weedel's Rheumatism Cure. They passed a pretty frame church, white with a matching picket fence, and even a schoolhouse.

"It's the kind of small town that you wouldn't mind living in," Jessie observed out loud as she drove past a bakery, restaurant and a millinery shop.

"There's the newspaper office," Linda said. "That must be where your old friend is working."

"I hope so," Jessie said, hurrying their horse into a quick trot that carried them up to the office, where she quickly jumped down and handed the reins to Ki. "I'll surprise him alone."

Jessie rushed up to the door, but to her dismay, it was locked. She looked around and then noticed a sign in the window that read, "CLOSED TEMPORARILY."

"It's closed," Jessie said, hurrying back to the buggy. "I just hope that we're not too late, that Max hasn't been killed or ended up among the missing."

"I didn't see a sheriff's office," Ki said.

"Then we'll find the first merchant we can collar and get to the bottom of this," Jessie vowed, hopping into the buggy and turning it around before applying the whip and sending them racing back to town.

They tied the buggy up before Atwater's Emporium and went inside to find a quaint little country store crammed with barrels of crackers, apples and pickles, as well as boxes of tinned goods and supplies of every description.

"Are you Mr. Atwater?" Jessie asked the smiling man behind the counter.

"Nope. Mr. Atwater died three years ago. My name is Bosley. J. P. Bosley. At your service, miss. So what can I do for you fine people today? My prices are fair, but I don't mind a little dickering. So look around and . . ."

"Mr. Bosley," Jessie interrupted, "we are friends of Mr. Max Maxwell, your editor. We have come a long way to see him, and now we find that his office is closed."

"That's because he's gone fishing," Bosley pronounced.

"Fishing?"

"Sure! Max is crazy about fishing. Does it most every afternoon except on Wednesday when he works on the paper."

"He only works on it one afternoon a week?"

"It's just a weekly. Couple of pages. You want to buy a copy, it'll cost you a nickle. I've got some ads in there and. . . . "

Jessie could not hide her vexation. "We came all the way from Texas under the impression that Max's life was in grave danger."

Boswell pursed his lips and his smile evaporated. "Well, to be perfectly honest, he is in serious trouble with Mr. Tower. And the smart money says that he'll wind up *feeding* fish instead of catching them one of these days."

"I see," Jessie replied in a low voice. "What can be done?"

"Someone needs to kill Gordon Tower and his two bloodthirsty sons. That would probably take care of it."

"Anything short of that?"

"Max has been to Sacramento several times petitioning the California State Legislature to outlaw hydraulic mining."

"Any success?"

Boswell shrugged. "It's like everything else. Money talks, and people like Gordon Tower have all the money."

"Where does Max usually fish?"

"Upriver about two miles there's a nice, deep pool. He has pretty good luck fly fishing just above it where there are some ripples."

104

"Thanks," Jessie said as she turned and started for the door.

"Hey, miss?"

Jessie stopped. "Yes?"

"Tell Max I sold two more copies of his paper and have his money waiting on the counter."

Jessie frowned. "I'd like to buy his last edition."

Bosley nodded. "Be two bits, miss."

Jessie reached into her jeans and paid the man a dollar. "The rest is for the directions and your time."

"My time ain't worth much," Bosley said, "but I'll keep the change anyway."

Jessie drove her wagon upriver, and when she saw the big, lazy pool of water, she knew that she was close. And since the day was warm and sunny, she said, "Maybe you two would like to go for a swim while I hike up and get Max."

"I'd like that," Linda said happily.

Ki glanced up the river, and Jessie could tell he was a little worried about her going on alone, so she said, "I'll be fine. Besides, the Tower family doesn't even know I'm around yet. There is no reason for them to cause me any harm at this point."

"A beautiful woman always attracts excitement," Ki said.

Jessie patted the six-gun at her side. "That's why I wear this, remember?"

The samurai nodded and forced himself to relax. He looked over at Linda, who was already standing beside the pool. "We don't have any swimming suits."

"Oh?" Jessie's eyebrows arched. "Well, then, if you want to swim and wash the dust off yourselves, I guess you'll just have to swim in the raw. Huh?"

Ki's eyes twinkled. "You don't give a man a lot of slack, do you?"

105

"Not when he's already stepped into the noose," Jessie said before driving the wagon on upriver.

She came upon Max less than ten minutes later. He was standing bare chested and knee-deep in the water, fly fishing and oblivious to everything except speckled trout.

Jessie pulled the wagon in and tied her horse to a sapling, then brushed her hair, straightened her blouse and went to pay him a visit.

Max had filled out a little since she'd seen him last. His chest, shoulders and arms were tanned, and he looked very fit and even a little muscular. When she had known him in San Francisco, he'd been pale and too thin, a man who rarely took the time to enjoy the out-of-doors. Now, he seemed to have made some great change, and Jessie wondered if he were the same man that she'd always found so interesting or if he had become a simple man content with simple pleasures.

When she was less than twenty yards from him, Jessie planted her feet on the shore and watched as he suddenly hooked a trout, then hauled it fighting to the riverbank, where he pounced on it like a big brown cat and shoved it into his creel. He was so busy and so excited that he still was not aware of her presence.

"Ought to be good eating," Jessie said.

Max jumped a foot, and his hand darted into his waders to snatch a derringer.

"Whoa!" Jessie cried. "I'm a friend, remember?"

Max blinked, and the fish fell forgotten between his feet. "Jessie!"

He rushed to her, throwing his arms out and hugging her to his bare chest. Jessie laughed into his ear and hugged him back, saying, "Max, you look wonderful!"

He pushed her out to arm's length, and his eyes danced

106

as he studied her closely. "And you look as ravishing as always, Jessie. I can't possibly imagine why some man hasn't swept you off your feet and married you by now."

"How do you know he hasn't?"

Max's smile evaporated. "Has he?"

"No," Jessie said, "but I wanted to see your reaction to the possibility."

"My reaction would be heartache," he said. "It would be the end of my fantasy."

Jessie stepped forward to kiss his lips, but before he could enfold her in a powerful embrace, she stepped back and said, "It was a long, hard and dangerous road to Pineville. But I've already heard that your life is in danger."

"I guess it is."

"Then why are you standing in the middle of a river fishing? Anyone could have shot you from ambush. Out in the water you make a perfect target."

"I do carry this derringer," he said, slipping it back into his rubber waders.

"What good would that popgun be against a Winchester?"

Max frowned. "I guess not a lot."

"You've got that right," Jessie said.

Max went back to his flopping trout. Pulling a knife out of his fishing creel, he mercifully dispatched the fish and dropped it inside. "I've only caught three fish so far this afternoon. Did you bring Ki?"

"Yes."

Max looked downriver. "Where is he? I've almost never seen him allow you out of his sight."

"He's in that beautiful pool of water just around the bend, swimming with a very pretty young lady."

Max blinked. "Is that right?"

"Yes."

"Things are changing," Max said. "Do you suppose they'd enjoy roasted trout for supper? Perhaps a little white wine and some roast corn?"

"I'm sure they would," Jessie said.

"Good!" Max picked up his fishing rod and started back toward the water. "With any luck at all, I'll have us a splendid dinner in less than an hour."

"What am I supposed to do?"

Max twisted around so suddenly that he almost lost his footing on the slippery rocks lining the riverbed. "I don't know. Sit on the bank and look pretty or undress and come over here for a swim."

"The water isn't deep enough."

"There's a pool just about a hundred yards farther upriver. Even nicer than the one down below."

Jessie thought about it. "I could use a wash."

"Then do it."

"And you promise you'll stay here and fish?"

He grinned and shrugged his shoulders. "Until I catch our supper I will. Can't say exactly how long that might take. Sometimes, I can't hardly throw my fly out quick enough for 'em."

"Then catch a few extra," Jessie said as she hopped back into the wagon and drove on upriver.

Max had not been lying when he told her that the pool upriver was a gem. Jessie shucked out of her clothing and found a rock overlooking the pool. When she dove into the cold water, her body made a clean cut through it, and it took her breath away as she swam to the bottom, then kicked up to the surface.

The river felt wonderfully refreshing, and she swam lazily around in it for nearly a quarter of an hour, sometimes diving to the bottom to pick up sparkling stones that looked like gold and silver nuggets. Actually, there did seem to be a fair amount of gold in the black river-bottom sand, and it made her think about hydraulic mining and the Tower family.

Jessie climbed out of the river, and as she headed for her clothes stacked on the rocks, she happened to glance up and see two thick-set and dark-haired men who were identical twins. They were quite some distance off but coming at her at a fast gallop, and she knew without question that they were the the Tower twins, Jason and Aaron.

She reached her clothes and, not bothering to dry, pulled on her pants and blouse. The damp blouse plastered itself over her breasts, and she tried to pull it away so that her shape was not so apparent, but it was hopeless.

"Jessie!"

"Over here," she called, buckling on her six-gun as Max, his waders squeaking and slowing his progress, came bounding up the shore to stand by her side.

The twins didn't rein their horses up until they were almost on top of Jessie and Max. When they did rein in, their horses' hooves kicked gravel up at the two of them.

"What the hell is the matter with you!" Max shouted in a fury. "Haven't you got any decency!"

Aaron and his brother could not tear their eyes from Jessie's chest, and she felt her cheeks blaze. "I think," she said, "this pair could not *spell* decency, much less abide by it."

Max stepped in front of Jessie, and she saw that he was holding the derringer in his fist so hard that his knuckles were white. "Get out of here, damn you!"

"It's a free country," Aaron said, "and we was thinking about having a little swim ourselves. You know this is the best swimmin' hole for miles around."

"Well, it's taken!"

"Not anymore," Jason said, dismounting.

"Jessie," Max said, "why don't you go to your wagon and drive it out of here right now."

"Hey!" Aaron protested, "We ain't even been introduced yet!"

"And you're not going to be," Max said in anger.

"What's the matter?" Jason said, his voice taking on an injured tone. "You worried that your sweet little friend might like the company of real men?"

Jessie had heard enough. She drew her six-gun and pointed it at Jason. "Get back on your horse and both of you ride out of here right now."

"Say," Aaron protested, "this is a free country, and I reckon we got as much right to swim here as you do, miss. Besides, if we all went swimmin' together in the raw, you might like what you see. We grow 'em real nice and long in this country."

Aaron chuckled lewdly and gave a bump to his hips a couple of times. Jessie replied with a bullet that ricocheted up between his legs, clipping off his boot heel in the process.

Aaron shouted in anger and surprise, and then he started to reach for his own gun, but Jessie's second bullet exploded against his holster and the man threw his hands up, holster and gun half-torn from his hip.

"You!" Jessie said, gun now pointed up at Jason. "I'll put my next bullet through your stupid skull unless you turn that horse around and get out of my sight in a hurry."

Jason's eyes drained of their former lust, and his thick lips twisted with anger. "You may have big tits and a pretty face, honey, but you just made one hell of a mistake."

"That's for me to decide," Jessie told him. "Now get out of here the both of you, because my next shot will count."

Max raised his derringer and pointed it directly at Aaron. "She doesn't miss, but just in case. . . . "

"You bastard," Aaron hissed. "We should have finished you off months ago."

"You tried," Max said. "You hired men to do your dirty work. Maybe someday you'll grow up to be men enough to try it all on your own."

Aaron's eyes glinted with hatred, and he cursed before he and his brother whipped their horses about and rode away.

"So," Jessie said, "that's them."

"Yes, fine fellows, aren't they," Max said with contempt.

Jessie sighed. "I suppose that I've sort of attracted their attention now, haven't I?"

"That's one way of putting it."

"No matter," Jessie replied, taking the man's arm. "Did you catch us our dinner yet?"

"Not quite. I saw them coming when they were still a long way off, and I just dropped everything and came running."

"Well, let's catch the rest of our dinner together," Jessie said. "I've never fly fished before, so you can show me the right technique."

The worry in Max's blue eyes disappeared, and he said, "I'd like that very much, Jessie. I just didn't know that there was something that you weren't already expert at."

"There are many, many things that you can probably teach me, Max. For one thing, how a person lives on selling a weekly newspaper that must not bring in more than a couple dollars a month."

"Oh, that's easy." He chuckled. "You drink water instead of good whiskey and you catch a lot of fish."

Jessie laughed, and they continued back down the river.

★

Chapter 13

Max had roasted fish and corn over a campfire nestled against the cover of overhanging rocks and only a few yards from the river. And now, as they finished their meal and stretched out to digest their dinner, he seemed ready to talk about his troubles.

"I came here on a whim. I had just heard that there was this little weekly newspaper for sale in a decent and friendly Southern Sierra town. I was eager to escape San Francisco, and I guess I thought this would be a lark."

Max stared into the campfire. "When I arrived and people learned that I was interested in buying the paper, they were very honest. The last proprietor had written a scathing article against the Tower Mining Company and its hydraulics, and he'd been severely beaten and run out of town. His simple Washington printing press and enough ink and paper to put out a year's worth of weeklies were free for the taking."

"The townspeople must have wanted a voice very badly," Jessie said.

"Sure they did. And I appreciated knowing right up front that I would be putting my head in a noose. Still, I hadn't met Gordon Tower yet, and I had the illusion that I could

113

reason with anyone. I read the previous editor's indictment and thought perhaps he had been overly critical."

"But he wasn't, was he?" Jessie said.

"No," Max admitted. "If anything, he'd been too charitable. The Tower operation is a rip-and-tear enterprise that is out to grab every flake of placer gold it can find, then leave this part of the country a wasteland. They don't care about anything but a quick profit."

Max lapsed into a brooding silence, and finally Ki said, "Can anyone stop them?"

"I'm hoping we can," Max said. "But not with guns. What we need to do is convince the members of the California State Legislature that they must take legislative action to outlaw hydraulic mining."

"I should imagine," Jessie said, "that they'd only have to witness the destruction."

"It's not that easy," Max said darkly. "In the first place, the Tower Mining Company contributes very handsomely to several important state legislators. Gordon Tower is no stranger in Sacramento, I can assure you."

"Neither am I. Nor was my father."

"Good! I was hoping you'd say that," Max told her. "So what I think you must do is to get a few key legislators down here to see what is really going on."

"That shouldn't be so hard to do."

"I'm afraid you are wrong about that," Max said.

"Why?"

"Because no one wants to buck a powerful family like the Towers. And those that aren't directly receiving contributions are probably hoping to someday."

Jessie thought on that for some time before she said, "It would seem that we need a champion of the people and the countryside. I'll find one for you in Sacramento."

"I have a few potential candidates," Max said, his voice

sounding more hopeful. "I have a list of progressive men who seem honest and who might be willing to listen."

Max gave her the list, and Jessie surveyed the names. Most of them were unfamiliar to her, but because she was on a first name basis with the current governor and many of the legislators, she had a feeling that she would be able to find someone who would help them save Pineville and these Sierras.

"The thing of it is," Max said, "few of the legislators want to take the time to come down here. There aren't that many votes, and it's not a quick or an easy journey from Sacramento. Most of those legislators won't go anyplace if they can't ride the train."

"I'll get a few down here," Jessie vowed. "But in the meantime, I'm concerned for your life."

"I've survived so far."

Jessie turned to Ki. "I want you to stay here with Max. I'll be in no danger in Sacramento, but after seeing those two identical thugs, I'm sure that Max needs some help."

Ki nodded his head, but it was clear that he was not pleased. He never liked to leave Jessie without his protection. "How long do you think you might be gone?"

"A week or ten days at the most," she assured him. "I will leave first thing tomorrow."

"I wish you could stay awhile," Max said. "We could write beautiful prose together. Love sonnets and poetry for my weekly, which is due out in two days even though I haven't written word one."

"Then I think you had better get started bright and early in the morning," Jessie said as she picked up her things and prepared to depart for town and a hotel room.

Max shrugged his shoulders. "I'd be more inspired to write if you and I could spend a few hours alone together counting the stars."

Jessie laughed. "We wouldn't get past ten if I read your mind."

"Maybe not," he conceded, "but we'd have an awful lot of fun trying."

In the morning, Jessie prepared to ride north to Sacramento. She would use the same horse that had pulled the buggy down to Pineville; only she'd need a saddle, blanket and bridle.

"Let me do the negotiating with old Al Sanders," Max said as he headed toward the only livery in town. "He can be shrewd, and if he suspects that he's got you over a barrel or that you're richer than a pharaoh, he'll really ream . . . I mean, he'll really take advantage."

"Even the rich hate to be taken advantage of," Jessie said.

"*Especially* the rich," Max said dryly, "which is often the reason *why* they're rich."

Jessie smiled. "I try always to be generous, but my father taught me to reward performance."

"How well I know that," Max said as they walked alone. "Don't forget, I was his up-and-coming young executive for five years before he was killed."

"So why did you leave our company? You could have become one of the top people in the Starbuck enterprises."

Max shrugged. "I don't know."

"Did I say . . . or do something to hurt your feelings?"

"No, no," he said quickly. "It was that I found it almost impossible to take orders from the woman I loved. When you ordered me to do something, I found myself wanting to countermand the order just to prove the value of my judgment. Or to simply attract your attention, even if it was your anger."

Jessie shook her head. She had always wondered why this man had aborted such a promising career. After he'd left her employment, Max had worked for many different companies, but none of them had held his loyalty for long.

"So now," Jessie said as they neared the livery, "you have sequestered yourself in a little bitty town that is about to be drowned in mud and power. You've taken yourself completely out of the society you knew best and become a simple country editor."

"Yes," he said, "I guess I have sort of divorced myself from all the big money and big pressure of high-stakes executive decision making. And you know what?"

"What?"

"I don't miss it at all. I'm happier and healthier than I've ever been before in my life. I don't have two dollar bills to rub together, but that's okay. I eat simply, have simple pleasures like reading and fishing; I live the life of a monk. I feel good about myself—better than I have for years, and I'm respected here in Pineville."

Max halted for a moment and shook his head. "Believe it or not, Jessie, I'm considered to be Pineville's most eligible bachelor and number one citizen. I've been asked to become mayor."

"And did you accept?"

Max's smile died. "No."

"But why?"

"Because I didn't think I'd survive the term."

Jessie linked her arm through his. "And now that Ki and I are here, do you feel the same way?"

"I don't know," he confessed. "You just arrived yesterday, and I'm going to have to think about it. To be honest, I never allowed myself to believe you and Ki would really come all the way from Texas."

"I would have come all the way from China if I'd received that letter," Jessie said. "We're friends, remember?"

"Once, we were more than friends."

Jessie nodded. "Yes, we were."

117

"So why did that change?"

Jessie shrugged. "People fall in love, but sometimes they fall out of love. I just don't know."

Max turned and continued the rest of the way to the livery with Jessie at his side. "Maybe we can fall in love again," he said. "Maybe if I write hard editorials against the Tower Mining Company and we fight and win this battle to save this country, then maybe we'll both be heroes and fall in love again."

"I don't know," she said. "That sounds like a fairy tale to me."

"So I always liked fairy tales," he said. "And I'm not counting on anything happening between us. I'm just asking you to leave it open as a possibility. Will you?"

Jessie reached up and kissed his cheek. "Of course I will! You're still one of the most handsome men I've ever seen."

"And you are the most beautiful woman in the world," he said, "but let's stop adoring each other and see if we can buy a saddle and a bridle without you getting scalped."

"Yes," Jessie said, following Max into dim recesses of the livery.

Al Sanders was a cigar chewer and a tobacco spitter, but when Jessie had left her buggy horse here the night before she had been impressed by how clean and well ordered the livery was and how sleek and fat the horses appeared.

"Howdy, howdy," Sanders said, rising from an oaken barrel and spitting a stream of tobacco into a stall. "You'll be needing your horse already, miss?"

"Yes," Jessie said, "and I think I would like to ride the horse rather than hitch up the buggy. You wouldn't have a saddle, bridle and blanket I could use, would you?"

The lids of Sanders's eyes narrowed. "Oh," he drawled, jamming his thumbs up behind his suspenders, "I reckon I would. Pretty nice saddle too."

"How much to rent it?"

"A dollar a day."

"That's outrageous!"

Sanders just grinned. "If you say so, miss. But that's the price. Take it or leave it."

Jessie scowled. "I need the saddle for a week at least. Why, I could *buy* an inexpensive saddle for ten dollars."

"Maybe, but not in Pineville."

Jessie tapped the toe of her boot impatiently. "What would you give me in trade for my buggy?"

Sanders spat again, scratched the back of his neck and said, "I'd trade you for the saddle, I guess."

Even Max, normally the most mild-tempered of men, was incensed. "That's common thievery!"

"Mr. Maxwell, you run your paper and I don't tell you how. Now don't you go telling me how to run my livery."

Jessie sighed. It wasn't the money that she objected to, because she had more money than she could ever spend, but it was the principle of the thing.

"I'll trade you my buggy for the saddle and one hundred dollars."

"I don't have a hundred dollars."

"Then the buggy and seventy-five dollars, tops."

"Fifty and you got a deal," Sanders drawled.

"This is outrageous."

"I know," the man said, "but you're already rich, and I'm just trying to make enough money to feed my own face."

Jessie stared at the man, and then she burst out laughing. When she finally caught her breath, she said, "It would have been a lot more straightforward if you'd just have told me that you knew who I was in the first place."

"Maybe," Sanders said, "but it wouldn't have been near the fun. Now, I'll saddle that horse of yours and you write

119

me up a bill of sale for the buggy and we're through talking business."

Jessie nodded. She found a piece of paper and pencil, scribbled out the bill of sale, and within fifteen minutes, she was tying her saddlebags on her horse and climbing into the saddle.

She rode back down the street to the hotel where they'd spent the night, to say good-bye to Linda and the samurai.

"Linda, you should just rest. Ki, please spend your time watching over Max. I have a bad feeling that our little confrontation yesterday by the swimming hole might just have precipitated some nastiness on their parts—or worse."

"I will do as you say," Ki told her. "But watch yourself."

Jessie nodded and when Max came over and laid his hand on her thigh, she bent and kissed him. "Be careful and write well."

"I will," he said. "And by the time you return with some of our esteemed legislators, I'll have an eyeful for them to read."

Jessie believed him, and with a wave of her hand, she reined away and headed north toward the state capital.

★

Chapter 14

Sacramento's beginnings dated back to 1839, when John Augustus Sutter, a Swiss, had founded his settlement at the junction of the American and the Sacramento Rivers. Sutter's Fort, as it was known for the next decade, prospered, and had gold not been discovered at Sutter's Mill, Sutter might have died a very happy and rich land and cattle owner. But with the cry of gold came thousands of argonauts, who quickly confiscated Sutter's land, cattle, sheep and even the fruit from his orchards and the grain from his fields.

By the mid-1850s, Sutter was financially ruined, but Sacramento was booming because of its strategic location as the terminus for the Overland Trail immigrants. Sacramento was also at the hub of river distribution, where it could provide men and supply ships easy passage to San Francisco or north to Marysville, which was the jumping point for the northern Sierra diggings, or southward to Stockton, from which the southern gold mines were supplied.

In the years since the Comstock discovery in 1859 and the decline of gold production throughout the Sierras, the rich agricultural lands of the Central and San Joaquin Valleys had already begun to promise an even greater reward than the played-out Sierra mining claims. And as Jessie rode northwest across the fertile valleys, she saw thousands of acres of barley, wheat, alfalfa and corn. There were farms by the hundreds, and when she rode past them, she could see that they were prospering. The houses were freshly white-washed, the barns and fences were in good repair, and there were chickens, geese and sleek milk cows in every yard. It was very much unlike the poor soddies that dotted the land-scape of the Northern Plains or the rundown, hardscrabble shanties of West Texas. Here, the land was rich and it fed its owners very well.

At the confluence of the Sacramento and American rivers, Jessie approached the capital city and was amazed at how fast it had grown in just the eighteen months since she and Ki had boarded a train there for Cheyenne, Wyoming. Everywhere she looked she saw commerce and traffic. Wagons were loaded fifteen feet high with produce and hay, while huge cargo ships from San Francisco and points around the globe were docked at the wharves, being loaded with agricultural produce and unloaded of a million and one supplies and luxuries for distribution up and down the great Central Valley.

In 1854, California achieved statehood, and Sacramento, to the great consternation of those living in San Francisco, became the state's capital. Fifteen years later, the Central Pacific Railroad chose Sacramento as its westernmost ter-minus, and the city that had once been Sutter's Fort was already well on its way to becoming the centerpiece of one of the world's richest agricultural centers.

Now, as Jessie rode steadily toward the capitol, she pulled the list of names she had been provided by Max and studied them more. There were several state senators and assemblymen whose names were familiar but only one that she could match with a face. "Anthony Montoya," she said, with a smile of remembrance. "Congratulations."

Montoya was a prominent and direct descendent of a Spanish grandee who had once owned a ranch that had encompassed over a hundred square miles of the valley. With the arrival of the the Mexicans, who ruled California for a short time before they themselves were displaced by the Americans, the Montoyas were stripped of their lands and herds. Unlike many of the Spanish nobility, who chose to return to Spain, the Montoyas remained in the area, and through sharp dealing and wisely helping the Americans overthrow the yoke of Mexico, they found themselves again with land and wealth.

Much to his family's horror, Anthony's father had fallen in love with and then married an Italian wine maker's daughter, who promptly gave the Montoyas a large brood of extraordinarily handsome sons and daughters.

Anthony was about the seventh son. He was called Tony and was perhaps the most handsome and dashing of all the Montoya children. Jessie had known him on a business basis several years earlier but had lost track of him when he had left the San Francisco area. Now, Jessie was delighted to learn that Tony Montoya had entered politics and been elected as a state assemblyman. And considering that there were many who still discriminated against anyone with brown skin, Montoya's feat was all the more remarkable.

"He is the one I will start with," she said to herself as she rode into the town and searched for a livery to board her horse before taking a room in the Capitol Hotel.

Jessie spent the early afternoon buying a dress and suitable clothes for the role she would have to play in this city of politicians. She much preferred to wear her tight-fitting riding outfit, but that would not do if she sought to gain the favors of important men.

It was almost six o'clock in the evening when she finally

123

reached the capitol, with its lofty dome rising more than two hundred feet in the air. Jessie entered the west wing of the impressive building, with its senate and assembly chambers, marble floors, great oil paintings and wine-colored velvet curtains. The heels of her new shoes sounded unnaturally loud as she moved down the almost deserted halls.

"Excuse me," she said to a rumpled, fiftyish man who stepped from an office with papers in his hand and had a very serious look on his face, "can you tell me where I can find the office of Assemblyman Montoya?"

The man peered over the top edge of his reading glasses. When he saw how beautiful Jessie was, his faint look of impatience and irritation vanished. "Why, yes, I can," he said. "In fact, if you'd like, I'll escort you there myself."

Jessie smiled. "Thank you. . . . "

"Senator Eastland. Robert Eastland. And who might you be, young lady?"

"Jessica Starbuck."

Eastland had started to give Jessie his arm, but now he froze. "Are you Alex's daughter?"

"I am. Did you know my father?"

Eastland nodded. "I met him a time or two. Of course, he was several years my senior and we had very little in common, but yes, I knew him. The man was quite a legend in San Francisco."

"He was that," Jessie said.

"Are you his . . . well, his heir?"

"I am. But I'm not here now on behalf of my company. I came to seek help for the little town of Pineville, California."

"Who?"

"Pineville," Jessie repeated.

"Never heard of it. Is that out in the Mojave Desert?"

"No. In fact, it's only about seventy miles southeast of

here. It's located on the Consumnes River. A small, quite lovely town. A family town, Senator."

"I see. Well, what is it about Pineville that you have come in need of?"

"It's threatened by a disaster caused by hydraulic mining practices," Jessie said bluntly.

The senator had bushy gray eyebrows, and they arched upward. "Come, come," he said. "Aren't we exaggerating just a little?"

"No," Jessie said, "we aren't. The Tower Mining Company is ruthlessly and methodically destroying that part of the Sierras, and I've come to see just what can be done to stop the Tower family before the beauty of that country is lost."

The senator's smile had died at the mention of the Tower family. "Gordon Tower is an old and valued friend of mine," he said stiffly. "I'm sure that he would never do such a callous thing as you have described."

"Then you should come back to Pineville with me and see for yourself," Jessie said. "In fact, I will count on you doing that."

"I will do no such a thing!"

"Why?"

"Well, because I haven't the time to go chasing out into the wilderness. I have a bad back, and I'm in no condition to ride a horse or a wagon that far."

"Bosh!" Jessie snapped. "I am almost sure you won't come because Gordon Tower pays you campaign money. Admit it!"

Eastland's jowls shook with outrage, and he even stamped his foot down on the marble floor. "I have had just about enough of this conversation. I don't care if your father was . . . was Abraham Lincoln! So good day, Miss Starbuck."

"Good day, Senator," she said. "I give you fair warning that, if you do not help us receive justice against this unconscionable practice of hydraulic mining, it will cause a public backlash against you. One that no amount of Tower money can deflect."

The senator stomped off down the marble corridor and disappeared, leaving Jessie to ferret out Montoya's office on her own.

It wasn't difficult. The assemblyman's name was stenciled above a door, and when Jessie entered, she looked through a waiting room to see Tony sitting behind his desk. Before him, a young woman was sitting holding an infant, so Jessie, not wanting to disturb the pair, took a seat in the waiting room.

She could not help but overhear the conversation between the assemblyman and the woman who, it turned out, had lost her husband in a railroad accident and was receiving no help from the Central Pacific in respect to financial recompense.

"I will take the matter up with the Central Pacific people at once," Tony promised. "I'm sure that once they realize their full responsibility to you and your child, you will be well provided for."

"Oh, thank you, Mr. Montoya!" the young woman said, sniffling into a lace hanky. "I tried to tell them that it was not my husband's fault that the brake line ruptured, but they wouldn't listen."

"I'm sure that they will listen to me," Montoya said. "Who did you say that you spoke to about this matter?"

"A Mr. Abe Beesley."

"And his title."

"Foreman of the railroad yard here in Sacramento."

"Ah, I see. Well, I can tell you right now that part of the difficulty is that you didn't go directly to the top and speak with the acting president of the operation, Mr. King."

"Oh, I was told he never deals with the public."

"He will now," Montoya said. "Starting tomorrow. You see, the last thing the railroad or any large corporation wants is to appear callous toward those who are harmed by its practices. I promise you that I will be heard and you will receive a just pension."

Jessie heard the young woman sob with relief and happiness. A few moments later, the assemblyman walked the widow out through his waiting room to the door and told her he would soon be in contact regarding a settlement.

"Nicely done, Tony," Jessie said before the senator could turn about and recognize her.

"Jessica Starbuck!" He laughed. "What a truly wonderful surprise!"

Montoya extended his arms, and Jessie gave the man a hug, then said, "You haven't changed at all, Tony. Still a man that takes charge, sees right from wrong and gets straight to the issue."

"And you," he said, "remain the most beautiful woman in all of America. Can I take you to dinner?"

"No wife to become jealous?"

"No wife would have me," Tony said with a laugh.

"I don't believe that for a moment," Jessie said, "and of course I will have dinner with you. When?"

"Why not tonight?"

"Yes," Jessie said, "why not?"

They had had a wonderful dinner at a marina, with the light of torches dancing on the rippling water and a marimba player that could handle any and all requests.

"You still have not told me why you are in Sacramento," Tony said. "I have told you everything about myself, and we have talked about many things but not why you are here."

Jessie raised her glass, which was instantly refilled with French champagne. "I'm almost afraid to tell you after what I experienced with a Senator Eastland only a few minutes before I found your office."

"You had a disagreement with him?" Tony asked with surprise as he also sipped a refill of champagne.

"Yes."

"But . . . but why? He is one of the most powerful men in Sacramento."

"I was afraid that you'd say that," Jessie said with a frown. "We had a rather strong disagreement over the Tower Mining Company, run by a man named Gordon Tower. Do you know him?"

"Yes," Tony said. "I'm afraid I do."

"Then he is not a major contributor to your campaign?"

"Hell no! He hates anyone with brown skin, and he's done everything he can to cheat the Chinese, Indians and the Mexican people. He is very rich and very evil, that one."

"He certainly is." For the next thirty minutes, Jessie told the assemblyman exactly what she had seen on the road to Pineville and ended by saying, "If you haven't seen it with your own eyes, there is no way you can possibly imagine the destruction caused by hydraulic mining."

"Then I must see it at once," Montoya decided. "I will return with you as soon as I finish up several important matters of business. But it would help if we could also get several other legislators, hopefully more influential than I, who could go along."

"I agree," Jessie said, "and a reporter from the *Sacramento Bee* to take pictures so that everyone could see what is going on."

"Yes, exactly!"

"We have our work cut out for us," Jessie said, feeling more hopeful than she had in quite some time.

"I know. And the fact that many of the most powerful lawmakers are recipients of Tower money is going to make this a hard fight."

"But a worthy one."

"Yes." Montoya's dark eyes glinted with the upcoming challenge. "This might just be the cause that I've been searching for, the one that will give me a worthy reputation and propel me into the senate, perhaps some day even into national politics."

"You can bet that I'll support your climb however and whenever I can," Jessie said. "Just as long as you never forget that you are elected by the people and no one—not me or any other person—can buy your vote."

"Of course," Montoya said, raising his glass. "We drink to victory over the Tower Mining Company and the new laws I author, which will forever prohibit hydraulic mining."

"Yes," Jessie said, her glass tinkling against his.

A few minutes later, they left the marina and walked for a short way along the river, watching the boats and listening to the sounds of voices carrying over the water.

"Where are you staying tonight?" he asked.

"At the Capitol Hotel."

"Why don't you stay with me?"

Jessie laughed. "And how would that look? Everyone would claim you were helping me because of a romantic involvement."

"They would be partly right, I'll admit."

"No," Jessie said, "it would hurt our cause."

"Then what about finding a nice, private little nook somewhere close and making love in the moonlight?"

Jessie could feel the champagne firing her blood, and the man beside her was not helping her cool down. "Is that what you'd like?"

"More than anything," he told her.

They stopped in the moonlight and Jessie turned to him. "And if I say no? Will you still be interested in helping save Pineville and other Sierra communities from being destroyed?"

"Yes, of course. It is wrong what they are doing. I will fight them on principle."

Jessie took Montoya's hand and placed it on her breast. "Let's find a hiding place," she breathed.

It took them only a few minutes to locate a hidden place covered with grass and surrounded by bushes. Jessie and the handsome assemblyman quickly undressed, and Montoya spread his coat on the ground for her to lie upon.

Lying on her back, looking up at Montoya and the stars, Jessie sighed with contentment. "Take me," she whispered.

Montoya wasted no time in mounting her. His large rod plunged deeply into her wet honey pot, and his mouth found her lush breasts.

"I always wondered what it would be like to do this to you," he panted as his hips surged in and out and she dug her fingernails into his buttocks, willing him to go deeper and harder.

"Well, now you know, Tony."

Jessie let the man have his way and his pleasure. Montoya was a good lover, and it took him a quarter of an hour before he arched his back and filled her loins with his seed. A moment later, bucking and groaning, Jessie found her own release.

Afterward, she held the man in her embrace a long time, feeling the gentle throb of his manhood as it slowly diminished.

"I liked the way you helped that poor woman and her child," Jessie whispered, "and I think right then I knew I wanted to do this for you."

130

He raised up on his elbows. "Come on! You mean this is some kind of a reward?"

"No," Jessie giggled, "unless the reward is for me. It's just that you were so encouraging and kind to her. I was impressed."

"And are you still impressed, with my other qualities?" he asked, nudging her with his hips.

Jessie raised her heels and locked them around Montoya's waist. "Even more so," she said.

He chuckled and kissed her mouth, and very soon, they were thrusting and making passionate love all over again.

★

Chapter 15

The next few days in Sacramento were filled with meetings as Jessie and Tony visited one legislator after another, trying to convince them to take a trip to Pineville to see firsthand the destruction being caused by hydraulic mining.

After one discouraging meeting, Tony escorted Jessie out of the man's office shaking his head. "It's clear that Gordon Tower has that one in his hip pocket."

"Yes, but at least we have an afternoon meeting with the governor. If we can sway him over to our side, then we'll gain a tremendous amount of momentum."

"I've scheduled a press conference right afterward," Tony said. "I hope I have something to tell them."

"You will," Jessie promised, "one way or the other, you will."

Governor Charles Whitehall was a tall, distinguished-looking man in his early sixties. He had made his fortune farming on the Sacramento Delta, and then he had gone into politics. A popular governor, he was considered to be strong-willed but not obstinate, and a man who would change his mind given just cause.

"The governor will see you now," a male secretary announced to Tony and Jessie.

"Here we go," Tony whispered. "We need this one pretty badly."

When they walked into the governor's office, Jessie's jaw nearly dropped to see Senator Eastland sitting across from the governor sharing a cigar. Jessie's heart sank, and when she glanced sideways at Tony, she could see that his spirits had also plummeted.

"Congressman Montoya, Miss Starbuck, it is good of you to come see me," the governor said, coming around his desk and extending his hand, first to Jessie and then to Tony. Jessie was surprised at how vigorous the governor was and how firm his handshake. Her own father had always claimed that he could tell more about a man by his handshake than he could from his looks.

"It's a pleasure to meet you," Jessie said. "The last time I was in California, you were running for office. Everyone said that you'd make a wonderful governor, and I've heard nothing but good things about you since."

The governor beamed. "Why, that's very kind of you," he said, his eyes lingering for just an instant on Jessie's voluptuous figure. "And, of course, I know all about your worldwide operation and about your late father. He was one of the great citizens of California, until he moved to that big ranch in Texas. His loss was felt in this state."

"He fell in love with a Texas cattle ranch," Jessie said with a smile. "And I confess, I did the same."

"But you still have a large staff in San Francisco and other offices all around the world, I'm told."

"Yes." Jessie had no doubt that the man who had told this to the governor was none other than Senator Eastland. "And I travel a good deal."

"I see." The governor glanced at the senator as if he expected the man to rise and at least acknowledge her presence. But Eastland did not look up or even smile. Jessie thought she saw irritation skim across the governor's eyes.

Jessie pretended not to notice that Eastland was studiously ignoring both her and Tony. He was sitting slouched in a chair puffing on his cigar, looking bored. Jessie would have loved to bat him across the side of the head.

Governor Whitehall momentarily turned his attention to Tony Montoya. "Tony, I hear very good things about you nearly every day. I think your reelection is a lead-pipe cinch and that you have a very brilliant future in politics, maybe even at the national level."

"As you have," Tony said.

"No," Whitehall said with a shake of his head, "I don't think so. Like you, I come from a very old and large California family. I'm not interested in living in Washington. I love this state and I think it's the most beautiful in the Union."

"I'm particularly glad to hear that," Jessie said, "because, right now, it is being destroyed by the Tower Mining Company and its hydraulic mining operation."

Senator Eastland bounced out of his chair as if it were on fire. "The hell it is!"

"Senator!" Governor Whitehall protested. "I must remind you that Miss Starbuck is a lady. I will not have you speak to her or any other lady in that tone of voice."

Eastland's face paled a little. He'd made a terrible mistake in allowing his temper to get the better of his good sense, and now he had to extract himself as gracefully as possible.

"I apologize," he said, all at once the model of contrition. "I sincerely apologize, and my only excuse is that, as I already told you, Miss Starbuck, Gordon Tower is an old and dear friend of mine. He is a man of immense integrity."

135

"He is a ruthless individual out to destroy the countryside if it will yield him a profit," Tony Montoya corrected.

Eastland swung around and jabbed his cigar in Tony's face. He was the junior legislator's superior and he meant to teach him a lesson. "The hell he is! And furthermore, if I hear that you're spreading vicious slander about Mr. Tower, I'll see that your repuation suffers for it, Assembly-man."

"You're on Tower's payroll," Tony snapped. "That means you have no credibility in this issue."

Eastland's fists clenched, and for an instant, Jessie thought that the old senator might actually strike Tony.

Apparently, Governor Whitehall did, too, because he said, "Gentlemen! Gentlemen! I do not see any point behaving like dock workers! Consider your positions! We are supposed to be reasonable, reasoning men. Control yourselves!"

Tony stepped back and Jessie could see that he was shaken. The senator looked even more upset, and Jessie saw hatred burning like a flame in his eyes.

"Now," the governor said, "I suggest everyone take a seat, and I'll listen to both opinions so long as they are not slanderous and without basis. And I'll brook no arguments or interruptions. Is that understood?"

Whitehall waited until they all nodded, and then he said, "Ladies first."

Jessie was as prepared as always. She reached into her purse and brought out the packet that Bill Fellows had sent her from San Francisco. "Here are the articles that brought me running all the way from Texas. And take a long, hard look at the pictures, Governor."

Governor Whitehall studied them with a grim expression. "I've never seen these before. Can the devastation possibly be this absolute?"

"It can and it is," Jessie said. "I've just returned from a place called Pineville. Some of those photographs were of an area only a few miles downriver from Pineville on the South Fork of the Consumes River. From what I am told, it is only a matter of time before Tower Mining moves up to the city limits and then circumvents it and moves higher into the mountains. You see, hydraulic mining requires enormous amounts of water and earth to extract only ounces of gold."

Senator Eastland could contain himself no longer. "Governor, those pictures are totally misrepresentative of what is actually happening down there. I've seen the operation and . . . "

"You told me you were never there," Jessie said in a hard and accusing voice. "The first time we met in the hall, you lied about this."

"I did not! I merely stated that my health would not now permit me to make an inspection of that operation. I neglected to say that I also know for a fact that such an inspection would be a total waste of effort."

Jessie shook her head. "Governor, you must listen to us. I saw a hundred acres of total destruction. Ten times worse than a wildfire ever left behind. You cannot believe your eyes at first when you see the mud, the broken trees, the silted river. Not only will this practice wipe out logging, but also the town itself because the river will be lost. And downriver, the farmers will discover, if they haven't already, that their fields will be covered with mud and their livestock will choke on bad water."

The governor expelled a deep breath, and Jessie noted that he could not tear his eyes from the pictures. Picking up one of the articles that Max Maxwell had written, his lips moved as he read it quickly, a frown deepening on his brow.

"Those articles are sensationalist hogwash," Eastland claimed. "Governor, I have seen the Tower operation, and I tell you it is employing hundreds of men. Men that were without jobs or even hope until Mr. Gordon Tower himself developed a method of extracting low-grade gold and silver. Metals that they pay taxes upon and that result in wages paid to voters."

The governor dropped the articles on his desk. Eastland had uttered the magic word. Voters. "Miss Starbuck. It seems that you and Assemblyman Montoya have entirely opposite views of the Tower Mining Company compared to those of Senator Eastland."

"Of course we do," Tony said. "Given the fact that Mr. Tower makes huge donations to his reelection campaign, what—"

"I object to that statement!" Eastland raged, jumping to his feet.

"Sit down, Robert," the governor said. "I'm sure that Mr. Montoya wasn't implying that you'd lie about what is going on down in Pineville."

"And I'm equally sure that he was," the senator snapped.

"Listen," the governor said, "I can't take the time to go see this. But I tell you what I'll do. I've a staff, and I'll send one of my best and brightest young assistants down there to check on things. If it's as bad as these pictures, then I'll personally visit Pineville. But until then, that's the best that I can offer."

Jessie could not hide her disappointment. "I think you should know that Pineville's last editor was severely beaten and then run off because of a highly unfavorable article he wrote about the Tower Mining Company and its hydraulic practices. You should also know that the current editor has had his life threatened on several occasions by the sons of Gordon Tower, two bullies named Jason and Aaron."

138

"Don't you believe a word of it!" Eastland cried. "Jason and Aaron are wonderful young men. They are both upstanding gentlemen of high moral caliber."

Jessie would have loved to have told the governor about how they had stared at her body and made their lewd and suggestive remarks as she'd held a gun on them. However, some things were better left unsaid.

Tony leaned forward. "Who will you send, Governor?"

"A young fellow named Alfred Perkins. I'm sure you know him."

"I do," Tony said without enthusiasm. "Would you object if a couple of my collegues also went along and saw firsthand what we have described."

"Governor, I object!" Eastland stormed. "What kind of an honest report would you receive if send a bunch of already biased friends of his? You'd get nothing but a bunch of bleeding heart rhetoric about Mother Earth being washed away and all that blather. You'd hear nothing about the hardworking men whose lives and fortunes—and those of their families—depend upon the Tower Mining Company for their economic well-being."

Governor Whitehall frowned. He stood up and walked over to his window, which overlooked the Sacramento River. "Rivers are the lifeblood of the West, Senator Eastland. But I'm sure that you know that as well as an old farmer like myself. Without clear, unpolluted water, the farmer can't survive and few others will make it either. If we destroy our rivers, the land they feed will follow as surely as night follows day."

"Yes, but . . . "

"So I'll tell you this," the governor said, turning around. "I value your integrity and your opinion. You are a good friend and a bad enemy. But I can't allow the Consumnes, the Sacramento, or any other river in this state to be fouled by mining or some other special interest. So if they are telling me the truth and you are not, then you and I are going to war. Is that clearly understood?"

Eastland was beside himself with anger. "Governor," he said, "I will not be threatened or intimidated. Not even by the highest ranking elected official in California. I have my principles and loyalties."

"Good," Governor Whitehall said a little coldly. "Then let's just make sure they are pledged to the right people and causes, eh?"

Eastland jammed his half-smoked cigar in a pewter ashtray on the governor's desk and turned for the door. "I resent this entire affair very deeply," he called back over his shoulder.

When he came to the governor's door, he turned and said, "I have every confidence that Al Perkins will support everything I've told you, to the letter."

"I hope so," the governor said, his eyes dropping back to the awful photographs that could not be ignored. "I sincerely hope so. Gordon Tower also contributed to my first campaign, but there were no strings attached."

"I believe you," Jessie said. "But I also know that not all elected officials possess your high level of integrity."

When she said that, she looked directly at the senator, causing him to whirl and leave, slamming the door.

The governor was silent for a long moment. "Mr. Montoya?"

"Yes, Governor?"

"I'm sure I don't have to warn you that you have just made yourself the second most powerful enemy in the state congress."

"I know that."

"Good." The governor shook his head. "Old Eastland has his faults, but don't we all."

"Yes," Jessie said, "but they do not include being bought."

The governor frowned. "Miss Starbuck, that is a very, very serious thing to say about anyone, especially a state senator whose service extends over the past twenty years."

"I'm very aware of his service to the state of California. But I've also seen what hydraulic mining is doing to the Sierras. Governor, politicians will come, and politicians will go. But the land—it stays on and on. Destroy it, and it may be gone forever."

Governor Whitehall nodded slowly. "I know that," he said. "I remain a farmer in my heart, and that is why I am sending Alfred Perkins. I trust his judgment."

"Good," Jessie said, "because once he sees what is happening with his own eyes, I'm sure that you will want to see it, too."

The governor nodded grimly and made it clear that the meeting was over. As Jessie and Tony were taking their leave, Whitehall said, "I will tell Perkins that he should go with you as soon as possible."

"How about tomorrow morning?" Jessie asked.

"Impossible. I need him here for the next few days on matters of great importance."

Jessie and Tony both knew it would be pointless and quite likely even counterproductive to argue that time was of the essence. So they thanked the governor and went out hoping that they had won the start of a victory.

Outside the capitol building, the press conference was waiting, but Senator Eastland had taken it over and was vigorously defending the Tower Mining Company.

"Anyone who has ever dealt with Mr. Gordon Tower or the Tower family knows that they would never do anything that would in any way deface or denigrate the land," he said with conviction ringing in his voice.

"Senator," the man from the *Sacramento Bee* interrupted, "just who is saying that the Tower Mining Company is destroying the land?"

"I am," Jessie said.

"And so am I," Tony Montoya said in a loud, firm voice.

The four reporters left the old senator and hurried over to hear Jessie and Tony's side of the issue. A few minutes later, a carriage pulled up. It was beautiful and pulled by a pair of matching white horses.

Senator Eastland, his face twisted with fury, entered the sequestered coach and slammed the door behind him. Jessie had just a fraction of a second to look inside and see who was waiting, and although she could not be certain, she thought that she recognized the square-jawed features of a Tower man, quite possibly even Gordon Tower himself.

★

Chapter 16

Gordon Tower stared across the dim recess of his coach and said, "Well, Senator, I heard enough at that press conference to know that we have a problem."

Eastland cleared his throat. "Nothing that can't be handled, Gordon. Nothing at all."

"Is that a fact." Tower managed a thin smile. He was a big man, larger than either of his sons, and his features were coarse and brutish. Men who saw him for the first time tended to form the impression that he was insensitive and not very bright. Actually, he was highly intelligent and sensitive enough to others that he could almost read their thought processes and then use them to his own advantage.

"There is a complication, though," Eastland said. "The governor is going to send his favorite aide to Pineville to report on your mining practices."

Tower's voice hardened. "Yes, that would be a problem. Can you control this aide?"

"I don't know."

"You had *better* know," Tower said, his hard voice cutting. "I've invested hundreds of thousands of dollars in hydraulic mining equipment, land and water rights and flumes. I'm sure as hell not going to lose it all because

143

some aide reports me to the governor."

"I'll talk to him right away."

"No," Tower said, "you'll buy his loyalty right away. I don't care what it costs; pay it."

"He might not take money," the senator argued. "I know the young man and he's scrupulously honest. That's why the governor values his opinion so much."

"Every man has his price," Tower snapped. "The only difference between them is the amount they must be paid. You find out this aide's price and pay it."

"Yes, sir," Eastland said, swallowing nervously. "Anything else?"

"Yes. How did Miss Starbuck get involved in this matter?"

Eastland shook his head. "I have no idea. She had several newspaper articles and some pictures which were pretty damning toward you."

"Were any of them written in Pineville?"

"Yes."

"Then it must be that the woman is a friend of Max Maxwell's. Damn that man! I should have listened to my boys and given them the okay to kill Maxwell months ago!"

"Kill him!" Eastland was very much taken aback by such talk. "Mr. Tower! The very last thing that you need now is to have your men kill that editor. If that should happen, it would only arouse the governor's ire, and he'd surely go there himself."

Tower considered this for a moment. "Very well, then I'll make one last attempt to buy Maxwell off."

"And if that doesn't work?"

"Then he will have a tragic accident," Tower said. "This is the frontier, Senator! Terrible accidents do happen every day."

The senator nodded and expelled a deep breath. "I can

tell you one thing, we'll be lucky to get out of this without some bad publicity toward your mining company. Hydraulic mining is just too damn destructive. I told you that right from the start."

"I need just five more years to make it reap fortunes for the both of us. After that, we'll quit."

"Will there be any wilderness left?"

"Oh, hell yes! My God, Senator, we've got the entire Sierra Nevadas to play with. You don't really think that we can wash an entire mountain range away, do you?"

"No, of course not. But I've seen what those hoses can do. I've seen them reduce a mountain to a mud puddle."

"I think you'd better be careful what you say," Tower growled. "And when it comes to this trusted and supposedly incorruptible aide of the governor's, then I want to make sure that he's in our hip pocket."

"But what if. . . . "

"If he can't be bought?" Tower smiled and shook his head. "I find that highly unlikely. But, if that were the case, then you'd have to find someone to eliminate him."

"Me!"

"That's right. I'm going back to Pineville and take care of our editor friend. Sacramento is *your* town. You fix whatever needs fixing here. Do you understand me?"

The senator nodded.

"Good!"

Tower had a beautiful walking stick. It was ebony-colored and had been made in darkest Africa, with a silver-headed eagle as a handle and a silver-tipped shoe that Tower liked to hear tap on the street as he walked. Now, he twice banged the eagle on the roof of his coach, and the vehicle came to a stop.

"Senator, I believe we have finished our little discussion on this matter. I will be sending you a very generous contribution when you have successfully completed your end of things here."

Eastland nodded and climbed down from the coach. "How much money can I afford to offer?"

"As much as it takes. I'm sure that a mere aide would be very impressed with, say, a thousand dollars. Wouldn't you, Senator?"

"Yes," Eastland said, wanting to tell the man that he would not have any part in murder. Either the governor's aide could be bought, or he couldn't. But Eastland would have no part in hiring someone to kill young Alfred Perkins.

Gordon Tower arrived at his mining camp the following afternoon, irritable and impatient.

"Pa, we got a big problem," Aaron said the moment his father opened the door.

"What now!"

"It's the big flume. There's been a break."

"Where and when?"

"Just this morning," Aaron said. "Come on into the office and I'll show you on the map."

"Damn!" Gordon swore. "Is Jason up there now?"

"Yeah, but I don't know if he can fix it. We lost almost all our water this morning, so the break has to be major."

Gordon stared at the unmanned hoses and the men standing around with nothing to do. "Let's get busy!" he shouted. "If you men can't find something do here, then get your lazy asses up to the break."

"We'll need them here if they get it patched up," Aaron said.

"Send 'em on up," Gordon snapped. "I won't have workers standing around with nothing to do."

"Yes, sir." Aaron shouted orders for the men to go help at the break, knowing that most of them would just hike up to the break and stand around there instead of here.

He followed his father into the large two-roomed log cabin that served as both their living and sleeping quarters and a working field office.

Tower wasted no time in reaching the huge map that was spread across a table. "Show me exactly where the break is," he demanded.

Aaron placed a finger on the map. "Right here."

"And are there men at the site fixing it right now?"

"Yeah. Jason left at daybreak."

"I want to see it myself," Gordon said.

"You look kind of tired," Aaron said. "Maybe you ought to just wait and rest a little while. I'm sure—"

"I want to see it! Get me a horse and get it saddled."

"Yes, sir!"

Gordon waited until his son was gone, and then he brushed his hands across his eyes. He had a payroll that was costing him hundreds of dollars a day. Losing downtime like this was like having one of his veins opened and letting his own blood spill on the floor.

Gordon glanced around the room and saw that it was filthy. There were dirty clothes piled on the floor along with several empty bottles of whiskey. A woman's bra was hung over one of the chairs, and it looked to Gordon as if his sons had had another one of their debaucherous parties with some of the local prostitutes they were forever recruiting with his money.

"Pigs!" he growled, noting the plates of decaying food and how the whole place stunk to high heaven. His sons, he had to admit, were pigs when it came to their own personal habits. He was sick and tired of hearing them make excuses for their own slovenliness, whining about how they'd never had a mother to teach them any better. But mother or not, they were going to clean up this rat-hole just as soon as the flume was repaired.

It was nearly sundown when Gordon arrived at the break in his flume and saw, to his relief, that the last timbers were being replaced and that the flume would be operational in the morning.

"What happened?" Gordon demanded.

"I don't know," Jason said, his face strained. "I just don't know."

"Had to be something big to knock the flume apart. You think that someone sabotaged it?"

"Could be," Jason said. "All it would take would be for two or three of them to toss a big log in there and it'd knock out a few planks the first time it came to a corner."

"Let's assume it was sabotaged," Gordon said. "And there's only one man that I know of in these parts with the balls to do something like that."

"Max Maxwell?"

"Who else?"

"We ought to stop farting around and just shake him down," Jason said.

"I agree, but it's a little too late for that now because a woman named Jessica Starbuck has the governor's attention. That means we have to make one more try to do things the easy way. Tomorrow, we'll go into Pineville and I'll try to buy Maxwell off."

"You already tried," Aaron said. "Offered him . . . what?"

"A thousand dollars. This time, I'll offer him five."

Aaron and Jason exchanged glances, and the latter said, "Why spend our money that way? Let's just kill him."

"I told you, I can't do that. Not unless it's made to look like an accident."

"We can do that," Aaron said. "Hell, pay us the five thousand."

"How would you do it?"

148

"I don't know," Jason admitted. "It would take some thought and planning."

"Then start thinking and planning," Gordon said, "just in case the man is a five-thousand-dollar fool."

"You mean corpse, don't you," Jason said with a cold grin.

"Yeah," Gordon said, "I guess I do at that. By the way, you boys left a hell of a mess at the cabin. I expect you to clean it up when we return."

"Yes, sir."

"And where'd you get the women this time?"

"From over at Columbia."

Gordon nodded. "Get an extra one for me tonight. Hear?"

The two twins smiled, and Jason said, "Already taken care of, Pa."

"Good. Now let's get out of here," he said as he walked stiffly toward his saddle horse.

The next day, the three Tower men paid a visit to the newspaper office, but it was locked and there was a scribbled note that read, "GONE FISHING."

"That bastard must like being poor," Jason said. "He fishes a hell of a lot more than he works."

Gordon Tower scowled and headed for his horse. "Let's go find him."

They had no trouble finding Max and Ki at Max's usual stretch of river. Ki was sitting on the bank watching Max's fly fishing technique, which was excellent, when he saw the three men approach.

"We've got company coming," he shouted.

Max swore and came wading onto the bank. He reached into his coat and pulled out a six-gun. "I didn't think you and the derringer offered enough protection," he said. "No offense."

"None taken." Ki shaded his eyes with one hand while his other slipped inside his tunic for a *shuriken* star blade. "But I don't think they've come to fight. If they wanted you dead, they'd hire someone to do it or else fire upon us from ambush."

"You're right," Max said. "Gordon is too smart to dirty his own hands with an enemy's blood. What he'll probably try to do is to buy me off."

"Hello there!" Gordon Tower shouted in greeting as he approached, flanked by his sons.

Max said nothing, and when the Towers reined in, he waited.

"Fish bitin'?" Gordon asked.

"They are," Max said.

"Good." Tower thumbed back his hat. "You know, Max, I envy you for the way you seem to find life so agreeable. Most of us work like dogs from sundown to sunset, but you . . . well, you just work a little bit and mostly you fish."

Max chuckled without warmth. "You could try fishing the rivers instead of destroying them, Gordon. Maybe if you spent more time in a pair of waders with a pole in your hand you'd have some appreciation of the effect silting and diverting rivers has on fish—and people."

"Maybe," Gordon said, "but the truth of it is, I like making money more than catching fish. And what I have in mind might make it possible for you to both fish and make money at the same time. Interested?"

"I always listen."

"Good, then why don't you tell your Chinese buddy here to take a hike? What I have to say is business."

Max shook his head. "I think you can say whatever you like in front of Ki. He's my friend."

Gordon's cheeks colored. "All right. Five thousand."

"For what?" Max asked with feigned innocence.

"You know for what!"

"But just so that I know for sure what you'd expect for your money, Mr. Tower. Five thousand for what?"

"For your newspaper business and the promise you'd leave Pineville and never return."

"Oh." Max frowned and scratched his cheek as if he were agonizing over the offer. "Well, you see, I just can't take your money," he said finally.

"Why not!"

Max shrugged. "I dunno. I'd rather live here and write a little and fish a lot. And if I sold out to you, well, I'd blow all the money anyway, and I'd hate myself for selling out this river."

"Did you sabotage our flume?" Aaron demanded.

Max turned his attention on the man. "Who, me?"

"Yeah, damn you!"

"I don't know what you're talking about."

Aaron jumped out of his saddle. "Well maybe I'll just beat your head in and then you'll remember."

As he started past Ki, the samurai stuck his foot out and tripped Aaron, who spilled headlong into the dirt.

"You yellow son-of-a-bitch!" Aaron screamed.

"Get him!" Jason hissed.

Aaron was fifty pounds heavier and two inches taller than Ki, so when he came rushing in, Ki did not try to stand up to the man but, instead, stepped sideways and drove a powerful sweep-kick into the man's side, just under his ribs.

Aaron's face went white, and he doubled up and sagged to his knees, his mouth silently opening and closing.

"Jason!" Gordon shouted. "Help your brother!"

Jason was just as big as his twin, and he was more cautious. Instead of rushing Ki, he came in feinting punches, and when Ki did not take any of his feints, he snarled and threw a haymaker that would have knocked Ki's head off had it connected.

But it didn't connect, as Ki ducked and pounded two lightning blows to the man's solar plexus and his belly. Jason staggered, and Ki's left hand slashed down and caught him at the base of the neck, driving him to the ground.

Gordon Tower was livid. "You yellow son-of-a-bitch!" he raged, his hand going for the gun at his side.

"Hold it!" Max shouted, raising his weapon and taking dead aim at the older man's chest. "Pull it and you're history."

Tower had just enough control to save his own life. He raised his hands, and then he said, "You're both dead men. I swear you are."

Tower reined his horse around and spurred away hard, leaving his sons gasping on the riverbank. To Ki, that showed just how hard the man really was inside.

"You'd better get on your horses and get out of here," Ki said, helping both men to their saddles.

When they were mounted, Ki said, "Your father is good at warning people about things. Well, I'm giving you a warning. Stay away from us or you'll be the ones that are going to die. Is that understood?"

Jason's lips twisted, and he hissed, "Mister, I don't know what you are or where you come from, but all those fancy kicks and punches you threw at me aren't going to stop a rifle slug. You're the same as dead."

In answer, Ki slapped the man's horse on the rump and sent it galloping away.

"They mean business," Max said as he shoved his six-gun back into his coat pocket and picked up his fishing pole.

"Well, so do we," the samurai answered.

★

Chapter 17

Gordon Tower had thought it all out by the time he and his humiliated sons had arrived back at the cabin.

"You both make me sick," he said contemptuously.

"Well, if you think you could have taken the Chinaman, then you should have climbed down from your horse and gone for him!" Jason raged.

"Shut up!" Gordon sat down behind his desk. "We need some professional help."

"Why!" Aaron said in anger. "Pa, we can ambush the two of them ourselves. Why bring in anyone else?"

"Because," Gordon said, "there may be an investigation or a hearing, and I want all three of us to have ironclad alibis so that we can prove we were nowhere around when Maxwell and his friend are killed."

Aaron and Jason exchanged glances. It was clear that they wanted to kill Ki and Maxwell themselves, and yet, they could follow their father's logic. "So who you got in mind to kill 'em?" Jason asked.

"I want you to go find the Castillo brothers and hire them to do the job."

"Yeah," Aaron said. "They've never failed us yet. How much do we pay 'em?"

"A hundred dollars a head." Gordon reached into his pocket and pulled out a thick roll of bills. He peeled off two hundred dollars and said, "If you spend this on whiskey or women before you pay the Castillo brothers, you boys had better keep right on moving because I'll send the Castillo brothers after *you*."

Aaron took the money and laughed, "Now, Pa, you know you wouldn't do that."

"Try me," Gordon Tower said. "Just take that money and blow it on women or whiskey and try me."

The laughter died in Aaron's throat and Jason gulped, because they only had to look into their father's eyes to know that he was not bluffing.

"Go find them now," Gordon said.

"But it's just an hour before sundown! Can't we at least wait until tomorrow?"

"No."

"Damnation!" Aaron groused. "I swear, Pa. Sometimes you treat us worse than dirt. And us being your only blood relatives. It's wrong."

Gordon stood up and sneered. "I treat you boys rough because you need a rough hand. You boys haven't given me one day of pride in your whole lives. You've messed everything up I ever set you to doing. I can't count on either of you to fix anything that goes wrong, and I don't know what's to become of things after I'm gone. I suspect that everything I've spent my life working to build will all be pissed away in a few years. And when it's gone, all you boys will have to show for it will be cases of the French disease and bad livers from too much drinking."

"Aw, Pa, that's no way to—"

"Get the hell outta here and go find the Castillo brothers!" Gordon raged.

Jason and Aaron headed out the door with their cheeks

blazing with anger and humiliation. They climbed back on their horses and spurred away, but after they'd ridden out of sight, Jason reined in.

"Hell, I'm feeling busted up from those kicks and punches I took."

"I don't feel none so good either."

"What do you say we spend the night in Pineville and go lookin' for the Castillo brothers tomorrow?"

"I got no money for a room or food," Aaron said.

"We got two hundred dollars," Jason reminded him.

Aaron's face paled a little. "You heard what Pa said back there! If we spend that money, he'll send the Castillo brothers after us."

"So we tell the Castillos the price that Pa is willing to pay is $150. They'll do it for that."

"Are you sure?"

"Of course I am! They're just a couple of broke half-breeds. Where else they going to earn that kind of quick and easy money?"

Aaron shrugged. "I guess you're right about that."

"Of course I am," Jason said. "So let's have a little fun tonight. We can maybe find a couple of women."

"In Pineville? Not very damn likely. There ain't been any whores there since the big strikes played out five, six years ago."

"Well maybe I just wasn't thinking of a whore," Jason said. "Maybe I was thinking of finding some town girls and showing them a real good time."

Aaron shrugged. "I don't think there's much chance of that," he said glumly. "All the women in Pineville are either married or engaged, or so ugly they'd have to pay us."

Jason chuckled. "Well maybe there's some new girl in town that we ain't even aware of yet. It's worth a look, don't you think?"

Aaron guessed it was, and since he was still aching from the blows that the samurai had delivered, he figured that he'd ride along with his brother to see what Pineville had to offer besides whiskey, a clean bed and a good steak dinner.

By the time they arrived in Pineville, it was sundown. After stabling their horses and getting a room at the Buckhorn Hotel for the night, they went down to the saloon and ordered up a bottle of whiskey.

"What kind of available women you got in this town?" Jason demanded of the bartender.

Pete Tulley shook his head. "You boys ought to know that this town rolls up the carpet at nine o'clock. You want excitement, you should have ridden on down to Fiddletown. I hear they got some new women there. Pretty ones that will dance on the tabletops and then take you in the back rooms and let you do anything you want to them for five dollars."

"Is that right?"

"That's right," Pete said.

Aaron elbowed his brother. "Maybe we ought to ride on over there. We could be in Fiddletown by ten o'clock."

Jason was considering that very thing when, suddenly, he saw a woman pass on the boardwalk.

"Did you see her!"

"Who?"

"Come take a gander," Jason said, heading for the door. "She was real good lookin'!"

Aaron gaped. "Damned if she ain't! Let's go make her acquaintance!"

"You boys better leave her alone," Pete said before they hurried off, "that girl belongs to that samurai warrior."

"That what?"

"That guy that looks like a Chinaman and—"

"She's *his* woman?" Jason said, his mouth open in disbelief.

"That's right."

"Well that's all the more reason for us to make her acquaintance, ain't it, brother!"

"Damn right," Aaron said with a wolfish grin.

Linda did not hear them coming until they were almost on top of her, and before she could act, one of them had his hand around her mouth and the other had grabbed her by the ankles and hoisted her up in the air. Then they were carrying her off down the alley.

"Now you just keep your mouth shut and relax, honey," Aaron said. "If you like that Chinaman, you're gonna love us."

Linda struggled mightily, but it was hopeless. Wild fear made her heart hammer in her chest, and when she managed to bite the hand that was muffling her screams, a fist exploded against the side of her face and she momentarily lost consciousness.

When she was roughly roused into wakefulness, her worst fears were realized. They were going to rape her. They had her down in a box stall, and while one was unbuttoning his pants, the other had her arms pinned down in the straw.

"You just relax and enjoy this, and no one will get hurt," Jason said as Aaron dropped to his knees with his manhood sticking out of his pants.

"No!" she cried. "No!"

"You screw Chinamen, you sure can't be very fussy," Aaron said, pushing up her dress until it was bunched around her slender hips.

"Please!" she cried. "Don't. . . . "

But Aaron's eyes were glazed with lust, and he tore off her underclothes and pried her legs apart.

Linda screamed and closed her eyes tight, remembering how the Indians had repeatedly raped her in the dirt after

157

killing her husband. She thought she was going to die then and she wanted to die now.

"No!"

But Aaron laughed and Jason panted, "Put it in her. What. . . . "

"Ahhh!" Aaron cried hoarsely as his spine arched and his hands reached behind his back for something.

Jason stared as his brother's face assumed a dazed expression and his mouth worked silently. "What the hell is wrong!"

Instead of answering, Aaron pitched forward onto Linda, and that's when Jason saw the star blade buried between Aaron's shoulders.

"Holy. . . . "

Ki watched the man reach for his gun, and when it had cleared leather, the samurai's hand flashed forward in a whiplike throwing motion.

"No!" Jason screamed a moment before the spinning wheel of death embedded itself in his forehead and blood poured across his eyes, turning his vision red and blurry.

Jason slapped at his face, tried to wipe his vision clear, but instead it became dimmer and dimmer until everything was black and he felt his heart quit.

Max Maxwell helped Ki tear the bodies away from Linda. "Those sons of bitches deserved to die slow. Not like that."

"There wasn't time for slow," Ki said, pulling Linda's dress down and raising her to her feet as she sobbed against his chest.

"It's all right," Ki said, over and over. "It's finished. You're going to be all right."

Linda struggled to gain control over herself, and when she succeeded, she said, "Just take me out of here."

Max heard voices and turned around to see Pete and a number of other people standing outside the barn gaping.

"You people, the Tower brothers tried to rape this poor woman and the samurai killed them. Anyone dispute that?"

Pete, who had raced to warn Ki and Max about Linda's fate, shook his head. "I seen what they was fixin' to do to that poor girl. And seen Jason go for his gun. They got exactly what they deserved."

Everyone nodded in agreement. Max said, "Just leave them as they lay. I want everyone to see them looking like dead animals so there's no doubt come burying time exactly what they had in their minds and why they deserved to die."

Ki escorted Linda out of the barn and to the hotel. As he passed the grim townspeople, one older man said, "Them Tower brothers didn't belong in Pineville. They were never a part of this community, miss. We want you to know that."

Linda sniffled. "I know. This is a gentle, decent town."

"That's right, miss. We feel awful about this. If there's anything we can do to make it up to you."

"Bury them!" Linda spat. "Just put them in the earth like they are. No fine words or fancy coffins. They don't deserve either."

"We'll do that," Max promised. "And if their father wants to dig them up, then he can do it on his own."

"Mr. Tower is going to come here and take this town apart," one man said, shaking his head. "Hell hath no fury like that man will have when he learns about them boys."

Max said, "If he wants vengeance, then let him come. And as for taking the town apart, better a showdown than watching helplessly as he poisons our river, then our fields and crops. I say it's time to fight."

"This ain't a fighting town," a man said. "We're all peace-loving folks."

"Sometimes," Max argued, "peace is out of the question. I've told you all along that we are doomed if we don't stand up against that man."

"I don't know," another said doubtfully. "If Mr. Tower decides to bring some of those rough men he employs, there's not much we could do against them. They're young and hard men. We're not equal to fighting their kind."

"Then maybe you'd better start taking target practice at first light," Max said with anger in his voice. "Because when Tower arrives, you can bet that he's going to raise hell."

As Ki escorted Linda back toward her hotel, he heard plenty of objections to Maxwell's hard fighting words. And it occurred to him that maybe, just maybe, he and the editor of the Pineville weekly would pretty much have to face Gordon Tower and his men all on their own.

Chapter 18

Senator Robert Eastland had a bad case of indigestion and his nerves were raw. He had not slept well for three days, and when he studied his face in the mirror, he thought he was looking at an old, old man.

Each day, the senator had waited for the moment when opportunity would present him with a chance to privately see the governor's trusted aide, Alfred Perkins, but that moment had never come. So now, as Perkins was making preparations to leave Sacramento and journey to Pineville early tomorrow morning with Jessica Starbuck and Assemblyman Montoya, Eastland knew that time was almost out. He had to speak with Perkins now, before it was too late.

"Ah, Alfred," he said, forcing a smile as he caught the young man alone, hurriedly stuffing papers into a leather attaché case, "I understand that you are taking a little outing in the country."

Perkins looked up, and he was, frankly, shocked at the senator's haggard appearance. But since Eastland was, next to the governor himself, the most powerful politician in California, Perkins smiled. "Yes, Senator. We are leaving at first light tomorrow morning."

Eastland closed the door behind him so that they could speak in privacy. He had practiced what he was going to say a hundred times, but now his pitch was forgotten. "I need to speak to you in private for a moment, young man. It concerns a matter of great importance to us both."

Perkins was a pink-cheeked young man with round wire-rimmed glasses, hair parted down the middle and a very correct and no-nonsense manner that bespoke his serious-ness. He was not the most congenial or attractive aide in the capitol, but he was the most intelligent and effi-cient.

"I am trying to prepare for the trip, Senator."

"Yes, of course," Eastland said, his cheeks flushing to be treated in such a cavalier manner by a mere aide. "I will come right to the point. The matter I wish to discuss directly concerns the Tower Mining Company and its practice of hydraulic mining."

Perkins blinked. "Yes?"

"Do you know Mr. Gordon Tower?"

"Not on a personal basis. But of course, I have seen him in this building on many occasions and I'm aware of his position."

"Good. Then you know that Mr. Tower is a man of impeccable credentials and very influential with many of our most powerful elected officials. I believe . . . " The senator cleared his throat and advanced a few steps. "I believe it is safe to say that Mr. Tower has even contributed handsomely to our governor's campaign."

"Not so," Perkins said, objecting quickly. "But I under-stand he promises to do just that when Governor Whitehall comes up for reelection."

"Exactly," Eastland said. "Now, the point of this is that Mr. Tower is being maligned by slanderous accusations con-cerning his practice of hydraulic mining."

"I'm going to visit his mining operation and write a report for the governor," Perkins said. "And I really must get—"

"But you see," Eastland pressed, "I am concerned that you will fail to appreciate the economic benefits that are being enjoyed by Mr. Tower's employees. Certainly, a large payroll in an area where there are few jobs for the people is a great benefit to everyone."

"I agree," Perkins said, "but we can't afford to devastate the mountainside and ruin our rivers. I've heard that the destruction is quite unbelievable. I've seen some pictures and . . . "

Eastland was getting desperate. It seemed obvious to him that this young fool was far too concerned about nature to be trusted.

"Listen, Perkins," he blurted, "Mr. Tower has invested tens of thousands of dollars in hydraulic mining. It is only now beginning to reap the rewards we—I mean, *he*, anticipated. You *must not* write an unfavorable report on hydraulic mining. For Mr. Tower's sake, but even more for all the people who depend upon the Tower Mining Company for their livelihood."

Perkins had always prided himself on his reserve and ability to keep a tight rein on his emotions, but what he was hearing now was quite unforgivable. "Senator Eastland, I have been assigned the responsibility of making a report for the governor on the Tower Mining Company and its impact on the environment and rivers. I intend to do that report without bias."

Eastland heaved a deep sigh. He had wanted more than anything to avoid putting his own neck in a noose by attempting a bribe, but now that seemed unavoidable. "I think you should know that I am financially prepared to help you make the proper decision on this matter."

"What?"

Eastland reached into his pocket and retrieved an envelope stuffed with five one-hundred-dollar bills. "There is five hundred. There will be another five hundred when a favorable report is on the governor's desk concerning the Tower Mining Company and the process of hydraulic extraction of gold from low-grade ore."

Perkins studied the envelope in the senator's hand, and then his lip curled down in a look of utter contempt. "Senator, get out of my sight," he said in a voice that trembled with indignation. "Get out of my sight and never speak to me again!"

Eastland reeled backward as if he had taken a physical blow. "Why you stupid, nobody little fool! I can break senators in this town, so what does that say about what I can do to *your* career!"

"Out!" Perkins shouted.

Eastland whirled, and when he reached the door, he said, "One word about this to the governor and I'll break you like a cheap wine goblet. I'll deny everything you said. It will be the word of a respected senator against that of an aide. You'll be driven from this building in disgrace."

Perkins was shaking so hard he could barely finish stuffing the papers into his attaché case. "The report will be an honest evaluation," he said. "But I think I can tell you that the governor and I have both discussed the matter, and if I find what we have seen in those newspaper photographs, then the practice of hydraulic mining will have no future in California."

"Make that recommendation, young man, and you will come to regret it for the rest of your days, however few they might be."

Perkins blinked behind his wire-rimmed spectacles. Had he actually heard the senator correctly? Had a senator really threatened his life?

Perkins looked up with astonishment and disbelief, but the most powerful senator in the state was already gone.

Perkins removed his glasses and placed them carefully on his desk. He could hear his heart pounding in his thin chest, and when he rubbed his hands together, his palms were moist with the sweat of fear.

"He *did* threaten my life," Perkins said out loud. "I heard it and it was a threat."

Perkins made himself sit down and take several deep breaths in an effort to calm himself. What should he do? If he accused the senator of attempting to bribe him and, failing that, threatening his life, Eastland would deny everything and he would be believed over a mere aide. But, on the other hand, to do nothing was taking a terrible risk.

"Think calmly," he told himself. "Act with intelligence."

Perkins remained seated and perfectly still for ten minutes, and when he was sure that he was being rational, he decided that the best thing to do would be to keep his own counsel and wait until he actually saw the Tower mining operation. Perhaps, as the senator claimed, reports of its destructiveness were totally blown out of proportion. If that were the case, he could write a report that emphasized the economic benefits of the operation and recommend that it be allowed to continue.

"Yes," he said to himself. "That would be most excellent. But I don't think that's what I'll find. And I don't think that Eastland or Gordon Tower believe it either, or they wouldn't have tried to bribe me."

Perkins shook his head and willed himself to stand on his own two feet. An overriding impulse told him to go find Governor Whitehall and tell him exactly what had happened. But Whitehall probably wouldn't believe it either, and without proof, what could the governor do? He was too savvy to accuse the senator of attempted bribery without evidence.

"I should have taken the money as evidence," Perkins said. "No! It would be inadmissible. It could have been given to me by anyone and so would prove nothing."

Perkins decided to say nothing. He would meet Jessie and Assemblyman Montoya and whoever else was going to Pineville early tomorrow morning, and he would keep his mouth shut and his eyes and ears wide open. He'd write his report honestly, if he could summon the courage in the face of a real threat.

Perkins finished stuffing his papers into his attaché case. He was probably forgetting something, but he was too rattled to care. So closing his door and locking it on the way out, he headed for his apartment, knowing that he would have a very poor sleep this night.

Senator Eastland ducked into the Bullshead Tavern, aware that he was much too old and much too well dressed to be out in this rough waterfront section of town. The tavern reeked of stale smoke, cheap whiskey, urine and vomit. When the senator entered, everyone turned to stare at him and he felt sweat pop out on his forehead like beads of quicksilver.

He made his way to the bar, ordered a double shot of rye and tossed it down, feeling the fire burn his throat and corrode the lining of his belly. He almost got sick.

"Another," he choked.

"You sure?" the bartender asked. "You don't look so good. And I don't think you belong in here."

"I'm looking for Bede," Eastland hissed.

The bartender had started to pour another glass, but now his hand froze. "Why?"

"I have work for him! Now will you pour me another drink, dammit!"

The bartender poured, and this time Senator Eastland did not attempt to toss it all down at once. Instead, he sipped at the drink and bit the tip off a cigar. "Is he here now?"

"Who are you?"

"A man with money needing help. That's all I'm going to say."

"Let's see your money."

Eastland glanced around the tavern and saw that the other patrons had dismissed him and were otherwise occupied. He pulled out his wallet, keeping it close to the bar so that it could not be seen, then he opened it so that the bartender could see the thick sheaf of greenbacks.

"Is he here now!"

"One hundred dollars gives you the answer."

Eastland wanted to curse but thought better of it. He had come this far, and there was no turning back now, because if he left this dim hellhole, he'd not have the courage to return.

"Here," he whispered, shoving the money across the bar.

It was quickly removed. "That's Bede over there by himself. I'll tell him you want to speak to him privately."

"No!" Eastland lowered his voice. "I'll speak to him right there. I'm not going into the alley or a back room with you or anyone else in this place."

The bartender shrugged his shoulders. "Suit yourself."

Eastland moved cautiously over to the man, whose back was turned to him. In the poor light, he could see that Bede was huge and hulking. His shoulders were humped, and he was wearing a sailor's jacket, black or dark blue and made of wool. He wore a sailor's cap, too, but he was barefooted.

"Mr. Bede?"

The man turned only halfway around, and when Eastland saw his face, he sucked in his breath. Bede was a terrible-looking human, with a wild black beard, one eye gouged out and uncovered and a fist-busted nose that was flattened on his face.

The one eye stared at Eastland like a coal in a snow pile. "What do you want?"

"May I have a seat? I have work for you."

When Bede didn't say anything, Eastland, on the strength of the whiskey he'd consumed, took a chair across the table from the man. "I got your name from Gordon Tower. He needs a job done on a young man named Alfred Perkins."

When the man didn't respond, Eastland said, "Here's his address. He lives alone, and the job has to be done tonight because he's leaving tomorrow morning very early. Do you understand?"

Bede stared at the piece of paper. "How much money did Tower give you?"

Eastland reached into his pocket and retrieved the same envelope he'd used in his failed attempt to bribe Perkins. "Five hundred now, the same when Perkins is dead."

Unlike Perkins, Bede grabbed the envelope, opened it and counted the money. Nodding his head, he pushed himself to his feet and started to leave.

"Hey, wait!"

Bede stopped and turned. His lone eye stared through Eastland, who managed to stammer, "How will I know you killed him and. . . . "

"You pay me the rest here tomorrow night or I kill you too," Bede rumbled before he continued on out the door.

Senator Eastland leaned his elbows on the table and cradled his head between his hands. He didn't give a damn if people were staring at him.

"Bartender!" he croaked. "More whiskey!"

"Come get it yourself, damn your eyes," the bartender shouted.

Eastland managed to push himself to his feet. Only he didn't go for his drink but rushed outside, where he leaned up against the front of the tavern and sucked in deep drafts of cool, riverfront air.

"My God, Senator," he whispered to himself, "what have we done now!"

Almost as if in reply, a ship blasted its steam whistle somewhere far out on the Sacramento River.

Senator Eastland forced himself to move up the street, and he tried not to think of Bede's one terrible eye and of what was about to happen to Alfred Perkins.

★
Chapter 19

Jessie and Tony Montoya arose before the first light of dawn, and their rented carriage was waiting outside in the darkness when they emerged carrying their bags.

"It's too bad that at least a few of your colleagues couldn't break away and join us on this trip to Pineville."

"Yes," Tony said. "But at least we have the Governer's aide. I don't know Alfred well at all. He's quiet and not very sociable, but he's honest, and I think he'll report to Governor Whitehall that hydraulic mining is every bit as destructive as we have described it to be."

Jessie gave their driver Perkins's address, and they entered the carriage. It was going to be a long day, but they would be able to arrive before dark, and that was important to Jessie because she wanted Perkins to see the devastation as she had first seen it, with a weeping wall of mud where once there had been a mountain.

The carriage moved swiftly through the still-deserted streets of Sacramento, and when it arrived at Perkins's apartment, an old brick building only a few blocks from the capitol, Montoya said, "I'll go up and get him."

Jessie nodded, content to wait. From her window she could just see the first rays of dawn, and she stretched, trying to rouse herself to wakefulness. She was very eager to return to Pineville and see Ki and Max again. She worried constantly about them, afraid that the Tower family would make an attempt on their lives.

The minutes passed slowly, and Jessie watched the door of the brick building with growing impatience. Finally, she opened the carriage door and stepped outside, wanting to stretch her legs. She was just about to say something to the driver when she heard two gunshots and a cry of pain.

Jessie was wearing a dress, but her six-gun was in her purse, and she grabbed it and turned toward the brick building as a big, hulking man filled the doorway.

"Halt!" she ordered.

The response was two quick muzzle flashes from the man's gun. One of his bullets shattered the door of the carriage, and the other struck one of the spokes of the front right wheel.

Jessie's hand came up, and as the man was about to unleash a third bullet at her, she fired with calm deliberation. The distance was less than twenty yards, and she knew that her shot was accurate the moment she pulled the trigger. The big man in the doorway straightened, and his feet did a little dance as if he were a puppet on a string.

His gun exploded once more as he tried to bring it to bear on Jessie, and she shot the man again, this time knocking him back through the door. Jessie bolted for the doorway. The man she'd shot twice was alive but dying, and she saw the terrible expression of hatred in his glazing eyes.

"Tony!" she cried, racing to the staircase and then starting up to the apartments above. "Tony!"

When she reached the upper landing, she saw Tony lying on the floor, trying to climb to his feet. His right cheek was bleeding, but he appeared to have been struck by a club, gun or fist rather than a bullet.

172

"Thank God, you're alive!"

"Yeah," he said shakily. "But I'm afraid poor Al Perkins is dead."

Now Jessie saw the young man, and he was lying face-down in a pool of blood. She ran to his side and rolled him over. "Oh no!"

Perkins was dying. He'd taken one bullet in the chest and another in the shoulder. As Jessie held him, his eyes fluttered open and he whispered something.

"I can't hear you," she told him.

Perkins gasped and then he seemed to summon all of his fading strength to say, "Senator Eastland paid for this. Tried to bribe me. I refused. He . . . he . . . said I'd be . . . killed!"

Jessie looked to Assemblyman Montoya. "Did you hear that?"

"Yeah, but without proof . . ."

"Eastland killed me!" Perkins cried with his dying breath as his frail body spasmed and then went limp in Jessie's arms.

Jessie lowered the young man's head to the floor. Perkins was wearing his glasses and one of his lenses was shattered. She removed the glasses and said, "What a waste."

Jessie hurried over to Montoya. "Can you walk?"

"Yes. He hit me when I came in. I think he was on his way down the stairs when I arrived, and he jumped me when I reached the door."

"Come on," Jessie said, taking the assemblyman's hand. "If we can talk to the killer and get him to tell us who hired him, we can send Eastland to prison or the gallows."

They stumbled down the dark stairs to the doorway and knelt at the terrible-looking man's side. Jessie touched his throat to feel for a pulse, but it was gone.

"Damn," she whispered in frustration.

Montoya leaned weakly against the doorway. "Let's go see the governor," he said. "We both heard poor young Perkins say that it was Senator Eastland who hired this killer. If we can trace this man to where they met, we might still be able to get enough evidence to hang the senator."

"I suppose," Jessie said, though she doubted it very much.

Twenty minutes later, they were at the Governor's Mansion, a huge alabaster edifice surrounded by stately poplars. Jessie instructed her carriage driver to go directly to the door of the mansion.

In no time at all, they were allowed inside and the governor was sitting before them dressed in his robe and pajamas. When Jessie quickly told him about the tragic loss of his aide, Whitehall's expression turned bleak and he said, "Alfred was my right hand. I would have trusted him with my physical life just as readily as I did with my political life."

"He was honest to the end," Montoya said. "If he hadn't been, he'd have his life and his money."

"Tell me again exactly what he said as he lay dying," the governor ordered.

Jessie repeated the young aide's final, desperate words, and then she added, "I'm sure that the man I killed can be traced to some place in town. If we just find someone who saw him and Senator Eastland in the past few days, then that, coupled with Alfred's dying words, should be enough to send Eastland to prison for the rest of his life."

"Yes," the governor said, clenching his fists. "And by God, I'll not rest easy until he is in prison!"

Jessie touched the governor on the sleeve. "Young Perkins will have died for nothing if we let Gordon Tower continue to destroy rivers and mountains with his hydraulic mining. Won't you please come with us to Pineville and see what Alfred was going to see?"

Governor Whitehall slowly nodded his head. "I will," he vowed, "just as soon as Alfred is buried."

Jessie and Tony exchanged glances that were filled with hope. Unless Gordon Tower planned to kill them all, Jessie was almost certain that the days of raping the mountainsides with the practice of hydraulic mining were history.

Jessie and Tony spent only four hours tracking down the identity of Bede Roe. The man had been in jail for everything imaginable, and it was not difficult to trace him to the Bullshead Tavern. No less than the chief of police himself, under direct orders from the mayor of Sacramento, accompanied Jessie and Tony to that seedy tavern, where Jessie displayed a picture of Senator Eastland.

"Did you see this man and Bede together the night before Bede was killed?"

The bartender shook his head. "Never saw the man in my life. Who is he, anyway?"

"Senator Robert Eastland."

The bartender laughed coarsely. "My friends, maybe you haven't looked around at the other esteemed patrons of this establishment. Why, right over there with his head on the table is Governor Whitehall and beside him, on the floor covered with vomit, is Senator. . . . "

The chief of police was big and black Irish. He reached out and grabbed the bartender by the shirtfront, cocked his fist back and said, "You'll tell us the truth or after I've finished beating your face out of both your ears I'll take you to jail!"

The bartender's chortling laughter died in his throat, and Jessie could see that the man took the threat very seriously.

"All right! All right! So the senator was in here and spoke to Bede that night! So what!"

Jessie expelled a deep sigh of relief, and Tony Montoya

said, "So that means you're the man that can put the senator away for life."

"It ain't my business!" the bartender protested. "I don't want any part of whatever it is you're up to."

"Who asked you what you wanted?" the chief of police demanded, grabbing the bartender and propelling him out from behind the bar. "You're coming to jail, and you're going to testify to what you just said."

"And if I refuse!"

"You'll wind up feeding the fish."

"Oh," the bartender said, "well, in that case . . ."

Jessie didn't have to hear the rest and neither did Montoya.

The afternoon following Alfred Perkins's funeral, the governor called Jessie into his office. "As I'm sure you know, Senator Eastland has been arrested and charged as an accessory to murder."

"Will the charges hold?"

"I don't know," Whitehall admitted. "The testimony of that bartender is critical. I've even interviewed him myself, and he is not what you would call a convincing witness."

"But you believe him, don't you?"

"Oh yes," the governor said, "but I won't be on a jury. At any rate, at the very least this will have destroyed the man's career. I can't say that that pleasures me. Senator Eastland has accomplished many fine things for the state of California. He's been a remarkably effective legislator."

"But he went rotten on us," Jessie said.

"Yes," Whitehall said, "he did. Sometimes I think that elected officials ought to be under a two-term limitation. But that is beyond my limited sphere of influence."

"When can we leave for Pineville?" Jessie asked.

"Would tomorrow morning suit you?"

"Perfectly," Jessie said.

"Good. I've leaked my plans to the press. I think we'll have company."

"The more the better," Jessie told him. "Because once the destruction of a mountainside is witnessed, you and Assemblyman Montoya won't waste a minute writing legislation to outlaw hydraulic mining."

"You're very confident on that point, aren't you, Miss Starbuck?"

"Yes." Jessie changed the subject. "Governor, I hope that you'll make a statement to the press that Senator Montoya ought to be given a lot of the credit for whatever truths will be uncovered tomorrow afternoon in Pineville."

"I promise to do exactly that," the governor said, "and just between the two of us, it would not surprise me at all if the day comes when he's sitting in my governor's chair."

"Me neither," Jessie said as she headed for the door.

★

Chapter 20

Gordon Tower stood alone in the Pineville Cemetery, staring down at the fresh mounds of dirt that covered his sons. From a distance, anyone watching him would have assumed he was a heartbroken father paying his last fond respects—but they would have been wrong. Gordon Tower was silently cursing his sons for their stupidity.

"You dumb sonsabitches," he hissed. "By almost raping that young woman you've turned the entire town against me, and they're ready to fight."

Tower, his craggy faced twisted with bitterness, kicked dirt on the fresh graves. "I told you to hire the Castillo brothers, but instead, you came here and figured to pull the wool over my eyes again. Well, look what it got you!"

Tower kicked more dirt over the mounds, and then he spat on each grave before he marched out of the cemetery and climbed on his horse, which was being held by one of the Castillo brothers while the other one kept a lookout for trouble.

"Find the samurai," Tower choked. "Find and kill him!"

"What about Maxwell?" one of the half-breeds asked.

"He's mine," Tower hissed.

"And our reward for killing the samurai?"

179

Tower pounded his fist down on his saddle horn. "A thousand dollars each."

The Castillo brothers smiled and nodded their heads with satisfaction before they rode off to find and kill the samurai.

Ki saw the two wiry half-breeds coming, and something in the way that they held their rifles told him that this was not to be a social call. Ki was alone because Max and Linda were at the newspaper office working on the weekly edition.

The samurai rushed into the shack that Maxwell called home and gathered his bow and quiver of arrows. Because he had already expended his favorite, Death Song, he selected Chewer, so named because of its corkscrew shape that would drive into a man's belly and chew it to pieces.

The samurai stepped into the doorway as the riders drew nearer. He could see that they were at least half-Indian and perhaps even more. Their hair was long and black, like his own, only it was cut off straight at the forehead and held back out of their eyes by a bandana instead of the braided leather headband.

When the brothers were in arrow range, Ki held up his hand as a signal for them to stop. The Castillo brothers did stop, and the one who was a little shorter than the other reined his pony to a standstill and said, "Are you the one called the samurai?"

"I am."

"We have come to kill you, samurai."

"Then it is you who will die this day," Ki told them.

The Castillo brothers giggled a little at that, thinking it was a big joke. They slid off their ponies, and then they stepped behind them and dropped their rifles over their ponies' backs and opened fire.

Ki was caught off guard for one of the very few times in his life. He had expected the pair to be so confident that

180

they would not even worry about taking cover from a man who held nothing but a bow in his hands. However, perhaps the brothers had been warned of the samurai's skills and were being unusually cautious. At any rate, Ki found he had no target, and as the bullets began coming his way, he was forced to jump back into the shack and take cover.

The Castillo brothers were not wasteful men. They fired perhaps ten rounds into the cabin, and then they held their fire. "Come and fight!" one called.

"You come and fight," Ki replied in a loud voice.

The half-breeds split off from each other, each circling the shack. Ki assessed the situation and found it not to his liking. These were seasoned fighters, not hotheads. Ki nocked Chewer on his gut string and edged out the front door, then sprinted off to his right as bullets began eating space all around him. He reached some brush and flung himself down, feeling like a man being attacked by a swarm of hornets.

A moment later, he heard the faint sound of moccasined feet racing toward him, and he jumped up to see one of the brothers attacking with his rifle at hip level.

Ki raised his bow and arrow and let Chewer fly. The arrow, because of its corkscrew-shaped head, twisted meanly and made a hissing sound until it bit into the half-breed's gut. The man screamed and, incredibly, kept coming, although his rifle slipped from his hand as he grabbed the shaft of Ki's arrow and tried to wrench it free.

Ki ducked as the dying man crashed over him and then rolled over and over in the brush, still struggling to pull Chewer from his belly.

The second attacker unleashed two bullets, and one of them grazed Ki in the upper arm but did not strike bone. Ki grimaced and the arrow fell from his hand.

"Yiii!" the half-breed screamed as he drew his knife and threw himself at the samurai.

Ki barely had time to raise his bow and drive its razor-sharp end through the man's throat. The attacker crashed to the dirt, and Ki yanked his bow from the man's body and then headed for the nearby river to clean it off. He could still hear the dying Castillo brothers thrashing around in the brush.

Tough and brave, they had never fought a samurai before, and that had been their fatal shortcoming.

Ki washed his bow and flesh wound in the river, and then he sat down and wondered why the two strangers had attacked him without provocation. It had to be Gordon Tower who had sent them.

The samurai's eyes grew hard. Soon, he thought, I will have to kill that one too.

Gordon Tower dismounted before the newspaper office and tied his horse at the hitch rail with calm deliberation. He knew that he was acting rashly, but then, he'd tried being cautious and smart and it had not worked. So now he would simply kill the editor and claim that it was a matter of self-defense. And because he could hire the best lawyers in California, he would be aquitted of the charge and vengeance would have been satisfied.

But when he entered the newspaper office, he saw that, once again, his plans had been laid to waste, because Maxwell was not alone. There was a very pretty women in the office.

"What do you want?" Maxwell asked, glancing sideways at his coat and his gun, which hung on a rack well out of his reach.

"Are you the woman my boys died over?" Tower asked, his voice flat and emotionless as his eyes bored into Linda.

Linda stared at him. It was like seeing a faded picture of one of the younger men who had tried to rape her just days earlier. "You're their father, aren't you?"

"That's right. Now get out of here while you can."

"No!"

Tower walked stoically across the board floor, and his hand flashed in a short, powerful arc that terminated against Linda's cheek and sent her reeling across the room. "Get out!"

Linda tasted blood and her head was ringing, but she was clearheaded enough to know that this maniac was about to murder Max Maxwell.

"In my coat!" Max shouted.

Linda grabbed for the coat, and as Gordon Tower's hand stabbed for his own gun, Max threw himself at the much bigger man.

The two men crashed to the floor, and Tower grabbed Max by the throat and then slammed his head twice against the big printing press. Max slumped, and Tower rolled on top of him, hands still clenched on his throat as he began to pound the editor's head up and down against the floor in crazed fury.

"Stop it!" Linda screamed. "You're killing him!"

But Tower was insane with rage, so Linda grabbed the editor's gun from his coat pocket and, clutching it in both fists, aimed and fired at almost point-blank range.

The mine operator covered his face, and Linda shot him again, blowing away the top of his skull.

"Max!" she cried as she dropped the gun and ran to the editor's side. "Oh, Max!"

He was dazed but conscious, and she cradled his bloodied head in her lap. Her tears fell on his face as she cried.

That's the way the people of Pineville found Gordon Tower, Linda and their next mayor.

And later that evening when Jessie, Tony and the governor of California arrived in town, Governor Whitehall, his face grim and his voice strong with emotion, stood up on the bed of a wagon and addressed the people.

"Citizens of Pineville, today you have witnessed the death of men, and I have witnessed the unimaginable destruction of hydraulic mining. Let me say that we have both been appalled and shocked by what our eyes have seen."

The governor motioned for Tony to stand up and join him. "Assemblyman Montoya and I pledge to you that we will not only shut the Tower Mining Company down, but we will push through legislation that will insure that hydraulic mining never again is used against these beautiful mountainsides!"

Jessie listened as the townspeople cheered. She looked to Ki and knew the samurai was thinking it was time to go home to Texas.

Tony Montoya was surrounded by citizens, as was the governor, and Jessie thought that they both looked like the kind of men who could be national leaders if they ever had that aspiration. And as for Linda and Max Maxwell . . . she just had a feeling about them both. That they'd fall in love and spend the rest of their lives here in this beautiful town. Maybe he'd teach her fly fishing and she'd teach him a thing or two of her own.

Jessie motioned to the samurai, and when he came to her side, she said, "I know a nice, deep pool where we could cool down and watch the clouds roll over the Sierras."

"Is that what you'd like to do for the rest of the day?"

"Yeah," Jessie said, "because starting tomorrow, we've got a long journey back to Texas."

Watch For

LONE STAR IN THE DEVIL'S PLAYGROUND

106th novel in the exciting LONE STAR series
from Jove

Coming in June!

A *special offer for people who enjoy reading the best* **Westerns** *published today. If you enjoyed this book, subscribe now and get . . .*

TWO FREE

A $5.90 VALUE—NO OBLIGATION

If you enjoyed this book and would like to read more of the very best Westerns being published today, you'll want to subscribe to True Value's Western Home Subscription Service. If you enjoyed the book you just read and want more of the most exciting, adventurous, action packed Westerns, subscribe now.

Each month the editors of True Value will select the 6 very best Westerns from America's leading publishers for special readers like you. You'll be able to preview these new titles as soon as they are published, FREE for ten days with no obligation.

TWO FREE BOOKS

When you subscribe, we'll send you your first month's shipment of the newest and best 6 Westerns for you to preview. With your first shipment, two of these books will be yours as our introductory gift to you absolutely FREE, regardless of what you decide to do. If you like them, as much as we think you will, keep all six books but pay for just 4 at the low subscriber rate of just $2.45 each. If you decide to return them, keep 2 of the titles as our gift. No obligation.

Special Subscriber Savings

When you become a True Value subscriber you'll save money several ways. First, all regular monthly selections will be billed at the low subscriber price of just $2.45 each. That's

WESTERNS!

at least a savings of $3.00 each month below the publishers price. Second, there is never any shipping, handling or other hidden charges—Free home delivery. What's more there is no minimum number of books you must buy, you may return any selection for full credit and you can cancel your subscription at any time. A TRUE VALUE!

Mail the coupon below

To start your subscription and receive 2 FREE WESTERNS, fill out the coupon below and mail it today. We'll send your first shipment which includes 2 FREE BOOKS as soon as we receive it.

Mail To:
True Value Home Subscription Services, Inc.
P.O. Box 5235
120 Brighton Road
Clifton, New Jersey 07015-5235

10571

YES! I want to start receiving the very best Westerns being published today. Send me my first shipment of 6 Westerns for me to preview FREE for 10 days. If I decide to keep them, I'll pay for just 4 of the books at the low subscriber price of $2.45 each; a total of $9.80 (a $17.70 value). Then each month I'll receive the 6 newest and best Westerns to preview Free for 10 days. If I'm not satisfied I may return them within 10 days and owe nothing. Otherwise I'll be billed at the special low subscriber rate of $2.45 each; a total of $14.70 (at least a $17.70 value) and save $3.00 off the publishers price. There are never any shipping, handling or other hidden charges. I understand I am under no obligation to purchase any number of books and I can cancel my subscription at any time, no questions asked. In any case the 2 FREE books are mine to keep.

Name _____

Address _____ Apt. # _____

City _____ State _____ Zip _____

Telephone # _____

Signature _____
(if under 18 parent or guardian must sign)
Terms and prices subject to change.
Orders subject to acceptance by True Value Home Subscription Services, Inc.